She Couldn't Believe It.

In a couple of minutes she would be face-to-face with Durango Westmoreland...again. When she'd made the decision to meet him in person, she hadn't thought that delivering her news would be this difficult. Now that she was here, Savannah was having second thoughts about telling the man with whom she'd had a one-night stand that he was soon to be a father.

She shook her head at her own stupidity, asking herself for the hundredth time how such a thing could have happened to her. She was a twenty-seven-year-old woman who knew the score on men and birth control. Too bad she'd been too busy celebrating her sister's nuptials and taking pleasure in Durango's seduction to take the proper precautions.

To make matters worse, she knew next to nothing about the man who was her baby's daddy. The one thing she did know—judging from the memories that had haunted her since their passion-filled encounter—was that Durango Westmoreland was an expert lover....

Dear Reader,

Thanks for choosing Silhouette Desire this month. We have a delectable selection of reads for you to enjoy, beginning with our newest installment of THE ELLIOTTS. *Mr. and Mistress* by Heidi Betts is the story of millionaire Cullen Elliott and his mistress who is desperately trying to hide her unexpected pregnancy. Also out this month is the second book of Maureen Child's SUMMER OF SECRETS. *Strictly Lonergan's Business* is a boss/assistant book that will delight you all the way through to its wonderful conclusion.

We are launching a brand-new continuity series this month with SECRET LIVES OF SOCIETY WIVES. The debut title, *The Rags-To-Riches Wife* by Metsy Hingle, tells the story of a working-class woman who has a night of passion with a millionaire and then gets blackmailed into becoming his wife.

We have much more in store for you this month, including Merline Lovelace's *Devlin and the Deep Blue Sea,* part of her cross-line series, CODE NAME: DANGER, in which a feisty female pilot becomes embroiled in a passionate, dangerous relationship. Brenda Jackson is back with a new unforgettable Westmoreland male, in *The Durango Affair.* And Kristi Gold launches a three-book thematic promotion about RICH AND RECLUSIVE men, with *House of Midnight Fantasies.*

Please enjoy all the wonderful books we have for you this month in Silhouette Desire.

Happy reading,

Melissa Jeglinski

Melissa Jeglinski
Senior Editor
Silhouette Books

Please address questions and book requests to:
Silhouette Reader Service
U.S.: 3010 Walden Ave., P.O. Box 1325, Buffalo, NY 14269
Canadian: P.O. Box 609, Fort Erie, Ont. L2A 5X3

BRENDA JACKSON

The
Durango Affair

Published by Silhouette Books
America's Publisher of Contemporary Romance

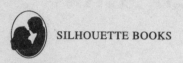 SILHOUETTE BOOKS

ISBN 0-373-76727-7

THE DURANGO AFFAIR

Visit Silhouette Books at www.eHarlequin.com

Printed in U.S.A.

Books by Brenda Jackson

Silhouette Desire

Delaney's Desert Sheikh #1473
A Little Dare #1533
Thorn's Challenge #1552
Scandal between the Sheets #1573
Stone Cold Surrender #1601
Riding the Storm #1625
Jared's Counterfeit Fiancée #1654
Strictly Confidential Atttraction #1677
The Chase Is On #1690
The Durango Affair #1727

*Westmoreland family titles

BRENDA JACKSON

is a die "heart" romantic who married her childhood sweetheart and still proudly wears the "going steady" ring he gave her when she was fifteen. Because she's always believed in the power of love, Brenda's stories always have happy endings. In her real-life love story, Brenda and her husband of thirty-three years live in Jacksonville, Florida, and have two sons.

A *USA TODAY* bestselling author, Brenda divides her time between family, writing and working in management at a major insurance company. You may write Brenda at P.O. Box 28267, Jacksonville, Florida 32226; her e-mail address WriterBJackson@aol.com; or visit her Web site at www.brendajackson.net.

ACKNOWLEDGMENTS

To Gerald Jackson, Sr., my husband and hero.

To my Heavenly Father who gave me the gift to write.

Love does not delight in evil but rejoices
with the truth. It always protects, always trusts,
always hopes, always perseveres.
—*I Corinthians* 13:6–7

One

Durango Westmoreland stood at the window and focused his gaze on the mountains as a dark frown marred his handsome face. He had awakened that morning with an ache in his right knee, which could only mean one thing. A snowstorm was coming. The forecasters were reporting that it wouldn't hit Bozeman and would veer north toward Havre. But he knew differently. His knee didn't lie.

There was definitely nothing scientific about his prediction but still, even with a clear blue Montana sky, he knew he was right. A man didn't live in the mountains unless he was in sync with his environment. The mountains could hold you prisoner in the valley whenever a snowstorm hit, and their snowslides struck fear in the hearts of unsuspecting skiers.

These were the mountains that he loved and considered home even on their worst days.

Durango's thoughts shifted to another place he considered home: the city where he was born, Atlanta. He often missed the closeness of the family he had left behind there, and although he would be the first to admit that he liked his privacy—and his space—it was times like this when he missed his family most.

He did have an uncle who lived near, although definitely not a skip and a hop by any means. Corey Westmoreland's breathtaking monstrosity of a ranch was high in the mountains on a peak that everyone referred to as Corey's Mountain. However, now that Corey had gotten married, he didn't visit as often. So Durango had become somewhat of a loner who was satisfied with enjoying the memories of his occasional visits home.

One such visit was still vividly clear in his mind. It was the time he'd returned to Atlanta for his cousin Chase's wedding and had met Savannah Claiborne, the sister of the bride.

From the moment their eyes had connected there had been a startling attraction. He couldn't recall the last time he'd been so taken with a woman. In no time at all she had turned his world upside down. She had actually charmed her way past his tight guard and his common sense.

Later that evening, after seeing the bride and groom off, everyone, still in a festive mood, had remained in the hotel's ballroom and continued to party, intent on celebrating the night away.

Both he and Savannah were more than a little tipsy and pretty wired up when he had walked her to her hotel room at midnight. And at the time, accepting her offer of a nightcap had seemed like the right thing to do. But once alone, one thing led to another and they had ended up making love.

That night his total concentration had been on her. Even now the memories of their one night together were tucked away and reserved for times like this when the claws of loneliness clutched at him, and made him think about things that a devout bachelor had no business thinking about—like a woman in his life who would always be within arm's reach.

"Damn."

He shook such foolish thoughts away and blamed his uncle's recent marriage for such crazy notions. Durango quickly reminded himself that he had tried love once and it had earned him a scar on his heart. That wound was a constant reminder of the pain he had suffered. Now he much preferred the easy life with just him and his mountains. He kept women at arm's length, except for when he sought out their company to satisfy his physical needs. Emotional need was as foreign a concept to him as sunbathing in the snow-covered Rockies. He had risked his heart once and refused to do so ever again.

But still, thoughts of Savannah Claiborne clung to him, did things to him. And no matter how many times he told himself she was just another woman, some small thing would trigger memories of that night, and along with the memories came the startling realization that she wasn't just another woman. She was in a class all by herself. At those times he could almost feel her lying beside him, beneath him, while he touched her, stroked her and coaxed her to take him deeper while he satisfied the pulsing ache within him….

Needing to get a grip, he forced his breathing back

to normal and compelled his body to relax. He turned around and headed for the phone, deciding to call the rangers' station. They were down one park ranger due to Lonnie Berman being in the hospital for knee surgery, and if they needed an extra hand, Durango had no problem going in.

As he dialed the phone he felt his control sliding back into place. That was good. That was the way he wanted it and that was the way he intended to keep it.

Savannah Claiborne stood in front of the solid oak door, not believing that she had finally arrived in Montana and that in a few moments she would come face-to-face with Durango Westmoreland again. When she had made the decision to come and meet with him instead of making a phone call, she hadn't thought that delivering the news would be difficult.

Now that she was here she was discovering that it was.

She shook her head at her own stupidity, asking herself for the one hundredth time how such a thing could have happened to her. She wasn't a teenager who hadn't been educated on safe sex. She was a twenty-seven-year-old woman who knew the score about birth control. Too bad she had been too busy celebrating her sister's nuptials to remember to take her Pill, which had left her unprotected and was the main reason she would be having a baby in seven months.

And to make a sad song even sadder, she knew very little about her baby's daddy other than that he was a park ranger and that, in her opinion, he was an expert at making love…and, evidently, at making babies, whether he had intended to make this one or not.

She also knew from the discussions she'd had with her sister that Durango was a devout bachelor and intended to stay that way. She had no plans to change that status but was merely here to deliver the news. What he did with it was his business. Her goal was to return to Philly and become a single parent. Getting pregnant might not have been in her immediate plans, but she definitely wanted this baby.

She paused after lifting her hand to knock on the door and released a deep breath. She was actually nervous about seeing Durango again. The last time she had seen him was when he had walked out of her hotel room two months ago after spending the night with her.

A one-night stand was definitely not her style. She had never been one to indulge in a casual affair. But that night she had gotten a little tipsy and emotional after seeing just how happy her sister was. It really was pathetic. She could never handle alcohol and she knew it. And yet she had fallen into the partying spirit and had imbibed a little anyway.

Since that night, Durango had haunted her dreams and had been the cause of many sleepless nights…and now it appeared he was partly to blame for interrupting her mornings, as well. Recently she had begun to experience bouts of morning sickness.

The only other person who knew about her pregnancy was her sister Jessica. Jess had agreed with her that Durango had a right to know about the pregnancy and that Savannah should tell him in person.

Breathing in deeply, she inhaled and knocked on the door. His SUV was parked out front, which meant he was home.

Savannah swallowed against the thickness in her throat when she heard the sound of the doorknob turning. Then the door opened. She literally stopped breathing when she looked into Durango's face, beyond his toe-curling handsome features to see the surprise that lit his eyes.

Standing tall in the doorway, wearing a pair of jeans and a Western-style shirt that covered his broad shoulders and muscular chest, he looked just as gorgeous as before—bigger than life and sexier than sin. Her gaze studied all the features that had first captured her attention: the close-cropped curly black hair, his chestnut coloring, well-defined mouth and intense dark eyes.

"Savannah? This is a surprise. What are you doing here?"

Savannah's stomach tightened once again; she knew what she was experiencing was probably the same effect Durango had on countless other women. She took a deep breath and tried not to think about that. "I need to talk to you, Durango. May I come in?" she said in a quick rush.

He quirked an eyebrow and stared at her. Then he took a step back and said, "Sure. Come on in."

Durango was certain he didn't possess a sixth sense; however, he found it pretty damn eerie that the woman he had been thinking about just hours earlier had materialized on his doorstep at the worst possible time to be in Montana. Although January was the coldest month in the mountains, February wasn't much better. Whatever she wanted to talk to him about had to be mighty important to bring her all the way to his neck of the woods in the winter.

He studied her for a moment, watched as she removed her overcoat, knitted hat and gloves. "Would you care for something to drink? I just made a pot of hot chocolate," he said, still at a loss as to why she was there and finding it hard to believe that she really was.

"Yes, thanks. It would certainly warm me up some."

He nodded. Now that she had removed all the heavy outer garments and stood before him in a pair of designer slacks and a cashmere pullover sweater, he couldn't stop his gaze from wandering over her body. It was as perfect as he remembered. Her breasts were still full and firm, her waist was small and her hips were nicely curvy. His gaze then moved to her caramel-colored face. It was as beautiful as before, even more so, he thought. And those eyes…

He inhaled deeply. Those hazel eyes had been his downfall. He had been a goner from the moment he had first gazed into them at the rehearsal dinner. And the night when they had made love and he had held her gaze when she had reached a climax, locking into those eyes had sent him over the edge. He had experienced an orgasm that had been out of this world. Even now he couldn't help but swallow hard at the memory.

But then all it took was a look at her sleek designer attire for Durango to remember that Savannah was a city girl. She had the words dignified and refined stamped all over her, although he could clearly remember when she'd tossed gentility out the window and displayed a distinct streak of wildness that one night.

Suddenly the memory of all they had done that night made every ounce of blood in his body race to his groin. Jeez. He had to get a grip. What happened to that control he had gotten hold of earlier? He was behaving like a horny teenager instead of a thirty-five-year-old man.

"Make yourself comfortable," he managed to say after clearing his throat. "I'll be back in a second."

He walked off, wondering why he was handling her with kid gloves. Usually when a woman showed up at his house unannounced he told them in a nice or not-so-nice way, depending on his mood, to haul ass and not come back unless he issued an invitation. The only excuse he could come up with was that since she was Chase's sister-in-law, he was making her an exception to his rule. And yet he had an unsettling feeling that there was something different about her, something he couldn't put his finger on.

When he returned with the hot chocolate he intended to learn the real reason for Savannah's surprise visit.

Savannah watched Durango leave the room. What she was about to do wouldn't be easy, but she was determined to do the right thing. He deserved to know. Who knows? He might end up being a better father to his child than her father had been to her, Jessica and their brother, Rico.

She smiled when she thought of her brother. Although he wouldn't like the thought of her being a single parent, he would look forward to being an uncle. And if Durango didn't want to play a part in his child's life, Rico would readily step in as a father figure.

Savannah sighed and glanced around, taking a real good look at her surroundings through the eyes of the photographer she was, and noticing just how massive Durango's home was, the spaciousness spread over two levels. The downstairs interior walls were washed stone, a massive brick fireplace was to her right and a huge built-in bookcase adorned one single wall. The bookcase was completely lined with books. She couldn't help but smile, thinking that she certainly couldn't imagine Durango spending his free time reading.

In the center of the room were a comfy-looking sofa and love seat that were separated by a coffee table. There were also a couple of rocking chairs sitting in front of huge windows that provided a beautiful view of the mountains. Wooden stairs led up to what appeared to be a loft with additional bedrooms. All the furnishings looked comfortable yet personable at the same time.

"Here we go."

She turned when Durango reentered the room carrying a tray with two cups of steaming hot chocolate. Even doing something so domesticated, he oozed a masculine sensuality that was playing havoc on her body. Her hormone level was definitely at an all-time high today. Even her breasts felt more sensitive than usual.

"Thanks," she said, crossing the room to where he stood.

Durango set the tray down on the table. Savannah was standing next to him, so close he could smell her perfume. It was the same scent she had worn that night. He had liked it then and he liked it even more now. He handed her a cup, deciding that he had played the role of Mr. Nice Guy long enough. He needed to know what the hell she was doing here and why she needed to talk to him.

He glanced at her; their gazes met. The eyes staring back at him were anything but calm. "What's this about, Savannah?" he asked smoothly, deciding to cut to the chase. She had no reason to show up on his doorstep in the dead of winter to talk to him, two months after they had last seen each other, slept together, made love…unless…

His eyebrows furrowed at the same moment as he felt a jolt in the pit of his stomach. For a moment he couldn't breathe. He hoped to hell he was all wrong, but he had a feeling that he wasn't. He wasn't born yesterday and was experienced enough to know that one-night stands only showed up again if they were interested in a repeat performance—or if they had unwanted news to drop into your lap.

His heart began to pound when he saw the determined expression on her face. All of a sudden, the thought that she had tracked him to his mountain refuge to bear her unwanted news made him furious. "Let's have it, Savannah. What's the reason for your visit?"

Savannah slowly placed her cup back down on the tray, tilted her head and met Durango's accusing stare. There was razor-sharp intelligence in the dark depths of his gaze and she knew he had figured things out. So there was no reason to beat around the bush.

She momentarily looked away, inhaled deeply and then met his gaze once more. He had no reason to be angry. She was the one enduring bouts of morning sickness, and she definitely wasn't there to make any demands on him.

Lifting her chin, she met his glare with one of her own and said, "I'm pregnant."

Two

Durango inhaled sharply when he experienced what felt like a swift, hard kick in the gut. She didn't say the baby was his but he knew damn well that was what she was insinuating. He made love. He didn't make babies. However, with the memories of that night constantly on his mind, anything was possible. But still, he remembered what she had told him that morning before he'd left. And with that thought, he summoned up a tight smile. "That's not possible."

Savannah lifted an eyebrow. "If you want me to believe that you're sterile, forget it," she said through gritted teeth.

He leaned back against the table, casually crossing his arms over his chest. "No, I'm not sterile. But if I remember correctly, the morning after you told me not to worry about anything because you were on birth control."

Unconsciously mirroring his stance, Savannah also

crossed her arms over her chest. "I was. However, I forgot to take the Pill. Usually missing one pill wouldn't hurt, but in this case…I seem to be the exception and not the norm."

"You forgot to take the Pill?" Durango's heart continued to pound and he shook his head in disbelief. The one time she should have taken the Pill she had forgotten? How much sense did that make? Unless…

"Were you trying to get pregnant?" he asked in a quiet voice.

He watched her jaw drop in shock, and saw the stunned look in her eyes before anger thinned her lips. It was anger he felt, even with the distance that separated them. "How dare you ask me that!"

"Dammit, were you?" he asked angrily, ignoring her reaction to his question. He'd heard of women who slept with men just for that purpose, either to become a solo parent or to snare a husband. And the thought that she had used him, set him up, raised his anger to the boiling point.

"No, I was not trying to get pregnant, but the fact of the matter is that I did. You fathered my child whether you want to believe it or not. Trust me, if I had been trying to get pregnant, you would not have been a choice for my baby's daddy," she said, snarling the words.

Durango's jaw tightened. *What the hell did she mean by that? And why wouldn't he have been a choice for her baby's daddy?* He shook his head, not believing he was asking himself that question. It wasn't like he wanted to be a father to any woman's baby.

"I think it's best that I leave."

Her words snapped him out of his reverie. His glare

deepened. "Do you honestly think you can show up here and drop a bomb like that and then leave?"

She glared right back. "I don't see why not. The only reason I came here to tell you in person was because I thought you deserved to know and now you do. I've accomplished my goal. I didn't come here to ask you for anything. I'm capable of caring for my child without any help from you."

"So you plan to keep it?"

Fury raced through Savannah. "Yes, I plan to keep it, and if you're suggesting that I don't then you can—"

"No, dammit, that's not what I'm suggesting. I would never propose such a thing to any woman carrying my child. *If* the baby is mine, I take full responsibility."

Her stomach twisted, seeing the doubt in his eyes. "And that's the problem, isn't it, Durango?" she asked, shaking her head sadly. "You don't believe that the child I'm carrying is yours, do you?"

Durango studied her silently for a moment, remembering everything about the night of passion that they'd shared. He knew there was a very strong possibility, a high likelihood, that she had gotten pregnant if she hadn't been using birth control, but he was still too stunned to admit anything. "I believe there might be a chance," he told her.

That wasn't good enough for Savannah. Whether he knew it or not he was questioning her character. Did he think she would get pregnant from one guy and try pinning it on another?

Without saying another word she walked back over to where she had placed her coat, hat and gloves and began putting them on. "There is more than a chance. It doesn't matter whether you want to believe it or not, there is something wonderful growing inside me that you put there. Not knowing your child will be your loss. Have a nice life."

"Where the hell do you think you're going?" he asked in a growl of both anger and frustration.

"Back to the airport to catch the next flight out of here," she said, moving toward the door. "I've done what I came here to do."

"One moment, Savannah," he grated through clenched teeth when she reached the door and opened it.

She turned around and lifted her chin. "What?"

"If your claim is true then we need to talk."

"My claim *is* true, Durango, and considering your attitude, we have nothing more to say."

Before he could draw in his next breath she walked out and closed the door behind her.

Durango stood at the window and watched Savannah get in a rental car and pull away. He was still reeling from the shock of her announcement and waited a tense moment to make sure she was out of sight before moving away from the window.

He glanced across the room to the clock on the wall and saw it was just past noon. He wished he could turn back time to erase what had just happened in this very living room. Savannah Claiborne had come all the way from Philadelphia to tell him that he was going to be a father, and he had all but told her to go to hell.

No doubt Chase would have his ass when he heard how shabbily he had treated his sister-in-law. Crossing the room, he dropped down into a leather recliner. It was so hard to believe. He was going to be a father. No way. The mere thought sent him into a state of panic. It seemed that babies were sprouting up everywhere in the Westmoreland family. Storm and Jayla had had twins a few months back; Dare and Shelly had announced over the holidays that they were expecting a baby sometime this summer; and when he had talked to Thorn last week, he had mentioned that Delaney and Jamal were also having another child.

Durango was happy for everyone. But babies were things other people had—not him. It wasn't that he'd never wanted a child; he'd just never given thought to having one anytime soon. He enjoyed the carefree life of a bachelor too much. He was a man who loved his solitude, a man who took pride in being a loner.

However, the one thing a Westmoreland did was take responsibility for his actions, no matter what they were. His parents had taught him, relentlessly drilled it into him and his five brothers, that you could distinguish the men from the boys by how well they faced whatever challenges were put before them.

Another thing he had been taught was that a Westmoreland knew when to admit he was wrong. If Savannah Claiborne was pregnant—and he had no reason to believe that she wasn't—then the baby was his.

Admitting that he was going to be a daddy was the first step.

He inwardly cringed at what he knew should be his second step—take whatever action was needed to take care of his responsibility. He checked his watch as he stood up. He wasn't sure what time her plane would depart, but if he left now there was a chance he might be able to stop her.

The woman was having his baby and if she thought she could pop up and drop the news on him without any further discussion then she needed to think again. She was going to have to deal with him even if the very thought of getting involved with a city girl made his skin crawl.

It didn't take much for him to remember Tricia Carrington, the woman he had fallen in love with four years earlier. She had come to Yellowstone on a two-week vacation from New York with some of her high-society girlfriends. During those two weeks they had an affair, and he had fallen head over heels in love with her. His uncle Corey had seen through Tricia, had picked up on the manipulator and insincere person that she was and had warned him. But at the time, he had fallen too much in love with her to heed his uncle's warnings.

Durango hadn't known that he'd been the subject of a wager between Tricia and her friends. She had bet her friends that she could come to Yellowstone and do a park ranger before marrying the wealthy man her parents had picked out for her. After telling her of his undying love, she had laughed in his face and told him she had no intentions of marrying him, because he was merely a poor country bum who got dirt under his fingernails for a living. She was too refined for such a dead-end union and fully intended to return to New York to marry a wealthy man with connections. Her words had cut him to the core, and he had sworn that he would never give his heart to a woman again, especially to a stuck-up city girl.

And Savannah was definitely a city girl.

He had known it the moment he'd seen her. She had looked high-class, polished and refined. It had been noticeable in the way she'd been dressed, the way she had moved gracefully around the room. She was confident and looked as if she could be married to a member of the president's cabinet. She was exactly the type of woman that he had tried to avoid during the last four years.

However, he refused to let her being a city girl deter from what he needed to do. Now that the initial shock had worn off and he had accepted that he had unintentionally aided in increasing the Westmoreland line, he would take full responsibility and take charge of the situation.

Savannah had not been surprised by the way Durango had handled the news of her pregnancy. However, the one thing she had not expected and could not accept was his questioning if he was her baby's father.

"Do you want to return your rental car?"

The question from the woman standing behind the counter snatched Savannah's attention back to the present, making her focus on the business at hand. "Yes, please." She glanced at her watch, hoping that it wouldn't be difficult to get a return flight to Philadelphia. And once there, in the peaceful quiet of her condo, she would make decisions that would definitely change her life.

One thing was for certain—she would have to cut back her schedule at work. As a freelance photographer she could be called to go any place at any time. She realized she would miss the adventure of traveling both in this country and abroad.

But now she would need to settle down. After all, she had prenatal care and visits to the doctor to consider. She would talk to her boss about assigning her special projects. She appreciated the fact that over the years she had built a pretty hefty savings account and could afford to take time off both before and after her baby was born. She planned to take six months of family leave time when the baby came.

The one thing she didn't want to do was depend on anyone. Her mom would be overjoyed at the news of becoming a grandmother, but since Jennifer Claiborne had finally found real happiness with a man by the name of Brad Richman, and their relationship seemed to be turning serious—if their planned trip to Paris this week was any indication—the last thing Savannah wanted was for her mother to devote her time to her. Her sister, Jessica, was still enjoying the bliss of being a newlywed, and her brother, Rico, would be busy now that he had started as a private investigator.

As Savannah stepped aside to let the next customer be served, she placed her hand on her stomach, knowing whatever changes she made in her life would be worth it. She was having a baby and no matter how Durango Westmoreland felt, she was very happy about it.

Durango stood next to the water fountain and took in the woman standing across the semicrowded airport. Damn, she was beautiful…and she was carrying a baby in her shapely body.

His baby.

He shook his head. What the hell was he supposed to do with a baby? It was too late to ask the question now, since the deed was already done. He sighed when he saw her head over toward the ticket counter, knowing what he had to do. He quickly crossed the room to block her path.

"We need to talk, Savannah."

Durango's words startled Savannah to the point that she almost dropped her carry-on bag. She narrowed her gaze at him. "What are you doing here? We don't have anything to talk about. I think we said everything, so if you will excuse me—"

"Look, I'm sorry."

She blinked as she stared at him. "What did you say?"

"I said I'm sorry for acting like an ass earlier. My only excuse is that your news came as a shock."

Savannah's eye's shot fire at him. "And…?"

"And I believe that your baby is mine."

She crossed her arms over her chest and glared at him, refusing to let go of her emotions and start crying. Since becoming pregnant she had turned into a weeping willow. "And what has made you a believer all of a sudden?"

"Because of everything that happened between us that night and the fact that you said it is. I have no reason not to believe you." A slow smile played on his lips. "So that settles it."

If he believed that settled anything then he had another thought coming. "Nothing is settled, Durango. Fine, you've acknowledged that I'm having your baby. That means you'll be one of the first people on my list to get an announcement card with pictures when it's born."

She turned to walk away and he blocked her path again. "Like I said, Savannah, we need to talk. I won't let you deny me the right to be a part of my child's life."

Savannah raised her eyes to the ceiling. An hour ago

he had been humming a different tune. "If I had planned to do that, I wouldn't be here." After a deep, calming breath, she added, "I came because I felt you should know and to give you a choice. I didn't come to ask you for anything."

She suddenly felt her face flush from the way he was looking at her. Was her hair standing on end? Were her clothes wrinkled? The flight hadn't been kind to her and she'd almost gotten sick from all the turbulence they had encountered while flying over the mountains. Her hair was a tangled mess and her make-up had worn off hours ago. By the time the plane had landed and she had gotten a rental car to drive out to his ranch, she had been so shaken up she hadn't cared enough about her appearance to even put on lipstick.

"Whether you ask for anything or not, I have certain responsibilities toward my child and I want to talk about them," Durango said. "You've done what you came here to do and now that my head is back on straight, we need to sit down and discuss things like two mature adults."

Savannah lifted an eyebrow and gave him a speculative look. What did they have to talk about? She'd already told him she wouldn't be making any demands on him. She swallowed thickly when a thought suddenly popped into her head. What if he planned to make demands on her regarding their child? Just last week there was an article in the Philadelphia newspaper about a man who had sued his girlfriend for joint custody of their newborn child.

Maybe talking wasn't such a bad idea. It would be better if they got a few things straight in the beginning so there wouldn't be any misunderstanding later. "Okay, let's talk."

* * *

When they reached an empty table in the airport coffee shop, Durango pulled out a chair for Savannah to sit down on and she did so, on shaky legs. Her gaze drifted over his handsome face and latched on to his full lips. She couldn't help remembering those lips and some of the wicked— as well as satisfying—things they had once done to her.

She glanced away when his eyes met hers, finding it strange that the two of them were sitting down to talk. This was the first time they had shared a table. They had once shared a bed, yes, but never a table. Even the night of the rehearsal dinner he had sat at a different table with his brothers and cousins. But that hadn't stopped her from scrutinizing and appreciating every inch of him.

"Would you like something to drink, Savannah?"

"No, I don't want anything."

"So how have you been?" Durango asked after he had finished ordering.

She raised her eyebrows, wondering why he hadn't asked her that when he'd first seen her earlier that day. He had picked a hell of a time to try to be nice, but she would go along with him to see what he had to say.

She managed to be polite and responded, "I've been fine, and what about you?"

"Things are going okay, but this is usually the hardest time of year for rangers."

"And why is that?"

"Besides the icy cold weather conditions, we have to supervise hunters who won't abide by the rules and who want to hunt during the off season. And even worse are those who can't accept the restrictions that no hunting is allowed in Yellowstone's backcountry."

Savannah nodded. She could imagine that would certainly make his job difficult. Jessica had said he was a backcountry ranger. They were the ones who patrolled and maintained trails in the park, monitored wildlife and enforced rules and safety regulations within the areas of Yellowstone. She shuddered at the thought of him coming face-to-face with a real live bear, or some other wild animal.

"You okay, Savannah?"

He had leaned in after seeing her tremble. Surprise held her still at just how close he was to her. "Yes, I'm fine. I just had a thought of you coming into contact with a bear."

He pulled back, smiled and chuckled. "Hey, that has happened plenty of times. But I've been fortunate to never tangle with one."

She nodded and glanced around, wondering when he would forgo the small talk and get down to what was really on his mind.

"What do you need, Savannah?" he finally asked after a few moments of uncomfortable silence.

She met his gaze as emotions swirled within her. "I told you, Durango, that I don't want or need anything from you. The only reason I'm here is because I felt you should know. I've heard a lot of horror stories of kids growing up not knowing who fathered them or men not knowing they fathered a child. I felt it would not have been fair to you or my child for that to happen."

He raised an eyebrow. "Your child? You do mean *our* child, don't you?"

Savannah bit her lip. No, she meant *her child*. She had begun thinking of this baby as hers ever since she'd taken the at-home pregnancy test. She'd begun thinking of herself as a single mom even before her doctor had confirmed her condition. She had accepted Durango's role in the creation of her child, but that was as far as it went.

"Understand this, Savannah. I want to be a part in *our* child's life."

She felt a thickness in her throat and felt slightly alarmed. "What kind of a part?"

"Whatever part that belongs to me as its father."

"But you live here in Montana and I live in Philadelphia. We're miles apart."

He nodded and studied her for a moment then said, "Then I guess it will be up to us to close the distance."

Savannah sighed. "I don't see how that is possible."

Durango leaned back in his chair. "I do. There's only one thing that we can do in this situation."

Savannah raised an eyebrow. "What?"

Durango met her gaze, smiled confidently and said, "Get married."

Three

Savannah blinked, thinking she had heard Durango wrong. After she was certain she hadn't, she couldn't help but chuckle. When she glanced over at him she saw that his expression wasn't one of amusement. "You are joking, aren't you?"

"No, I'm not."

"Well, that's too bad, because marriage is definitely not an option."

He crossed his arms over his chest. "And why not? Don't you think I'm good enough for you?"

Savannah glared at him, wondering where that had come from. "It's not a matter of whether or not you're good enough for me, and I have no idea why you would believe I'd think otherwise. The main reason I won't marry you is that we don't know each other."

He leaned in closer, clearly agitated. "Maybe not. But

that didn't stop us from sleeping together that night, did it?"

Savannah's eyes narrowed. "Only because we'd had too much to drink. I don't make a habit out of indulging in one-night stands."

"But you did."

"Yes, everyone is entitled to at least one mistake. Besides, we just can't get married. People don't get married these days because of a baby."

His lips twitched in annoyance. "If you're a Westmoreland you do. I don't relish the idea of getting married any more than you, but the men in my family take our responsibilities seriously." In Durango's mind, it didn't matter that he wasn't the marrying kind; the situation dictated such action. Westmorelands didn't have children out of wedlock and he was a Westmoreland.

He thought about his cousin Dare, who'd found out about his son A.J. only after Shelly had returned to their hometown when the boy was ten years old. Dare had married Shelly. His uncle Corey, who hadn't known he'd fathered triplets over thirty years ago, was an exception to the rule. Corey Westmoreland could not have married the mother of his children because he hadn't known they existed. Durango's situation was different. He knew about Savannah's pregnancy. Knowing about it and not doing something about it was completely unacceptable.

He had knocked her up and had to do what he knew was the right thing. Given the implications of their situation, getting married—even for only a short period of time—was the best course of action. He and Savannah were adults. Surely they could handle the intimacies of a brief marriage without wanting more. It wouldn't be as if he was giving up being a bachelor forever.

"Well, consider yourself off the hook," Savannah said, reclaiming his attention. "The only person who knows you're my baby's father is Jessica, although I'm sure she's shared the news with Chase by now. If we ask them not to say anything to anyone I'm sure they won't."

"But *I'll* know, Savannah, and there's no way I'm going to walk away and not claim my child."

For a quick second she felt a softening around her heart and couldn't help appreciating him for declaring her child as his. But she would not marry him just because she was pregnant.

She gave him a brittle smile as she rose to her feet, clinging on to her carry-on bag and placing her camera pack on her shoulders. The sooner she left Montana and returned to Philadelphia, the better. "Thanks for the offer of marriage, Durango. It was sweet and I truly appreciate it, but I'm not marrying you or anyone just because I'm pregnant."

Durango stood, too. "Now, look, Savannah—"

"No, you look," she said, eyes narrowing, her back straight and stiff. "That's what happened with my parents. My mother got pregnant with my brother. Although my father did what some considered the decent thing and married her, he was never happy and ended up being unfaithful to her. It was a marriage based on duty rather than love. He met another woman and lived a double life with her and the child they had together."

She inhaled deeply before continuing. "Dad was a traveling salesman and my mother didn't know that he had another family, which included Jessica, on the West

Coast. His actions were unforgivable and the people who suffered most, besides his children, were the two women who loved him and believed in him. In the end one of them, Jessica's mother, committed suicide. And I watched the hurt and pain my mother went through when she found out the truth about him. So no matter what you say, I would never let a man use pregnancy as a reason to marry. I'm glad we had this little chat and I'll keep in touch."

Chin tilted, she turned and quickly walked away.

"I'm sorry, ma'am, due to the snowstorm headed our way, all flights out have been canceled until further notice."

Savannah stared at the man behind the counter. "All of them?"

"All of them. We have our hands full trying to find a place for everyone to stay so they won't have to bunk here for the night. It seems that all the hotels in the area are full."

The last thing she wanted to do was sleep sitting up in a hard chair.

"You're coming with me, Savannah."

She turned around upon hearing the firm voice behind her. "I'm not going anywhere with you."

Durango took a step forward. "Yes, you are. You heard what the man said. All flights out have been canceled."

"Is this man bothering you, miss? Do you want me to call security?"

Savannah smoothed the hair back from her face. This was just great. All she had to do was look at Durango's angry expression to see he did not appreciate the man's question. To avoid an unpleasant situation, she glanced over her shoulder at the ticket agent and smiled. "No, he isn't bothering me, but thanks for asking. Excuse me for a moment."

She then took Durango's arm and walked away from the counter. She was feeling frustrated and exhausted. "I think we need to get something straight."

Durango rubbed his neck, trying to work away the tension he felt building there. "What?"

She leaned over and got all into his face. "Nobody, and I mean nobody, bosses me around, Durango Westmoreland."

Durango stared at her for a long moment then forced back the thought that she was a cute spitfire. Okay, he would be the first to admit that for a moment he had been rather bossy, which was unlike him. He'd never bothered bossing a female around before. He then thought about his cousin Delaney, and remembered how overprotective the Westmoreland males had been before she'd gotten married, and figured she didn't count. But this particular woman was carrying his baby and he'd be damned if she would spend the night at the airport when he had a guest room back at his ranch that she could use. He decided to use another approach. It was well-known within his family that he could switch from being an ass to an angel in the blink of an eye.

He reached out and took her hand. "I do apologize if I came off rather bossy just now, Savannah. I was merely thinking of your and the baby's welfare. I'm sure sleeping here in one of those chairs wouldn't be comfortable. I have a perfectly good guest room at the ranch and you're welcome to use it. I'm sure you're tired. Will you come to the ranch with me?"

His words, spoken in a soft plea, as well as his

ensuing smile, only made Savannah's blood boil even more. She recognized the words for what they were—smooth-talking crap. Her father had been a master at using such bull whenever he needed to unruffle her mother's feathers. And she was close to telling Durango in an unladylike way to go to hell.

And yet, spending the night here at the airport wouldn't be the smartest thing to do. She would love to go someplace, soak in a tub then crawl into a bed. Alone.

She met his gaze, studied his features to see if perhaps there was some ulterior motive for getting her back to the ranch. She knew from her sister's wedding that Durango Westmoreland was full of suave sophistication and he was an expert at seduction. And although the damage had been done, the last thing she wanted was to lose her head and sleep with him again.

She pulled her hand from his. "You really have an extra guest room?"

He grinned and her breath caught at his sexy dimples. Those dimples had been another one of her downfalls that night. "Yes, and like I said, you're welcome to use it."

Savannah toyed with the strap on her camera pack as she considered his invitation. She then met his gaze again. "Okay, I'll go with you if you promise not to bring up the subject of marriage again. That subject is closed."

She saw a flash of defiance in his eyes and then just as quickly it was gone. After a brief span of tense silence he finally said, "Okay, Savannah, I'll adhere to your wishes."

Satisfied, Savannah nodded. "All right, then. I'll go with you."

"Good." He took the carry-on bag from her hand. "Come on, I'm parked right out front."

As Durango led her out of the terminal, he decided that what Savannah didn't know was that before she left to return home to Philadelphia, he and she would be man and wife.

"Here we are," Durango said, leading Savannah into a guest room a half hour later. "I have a couple of other rooms but I think you'll like this one the best."

Savannah nodded as she glanced around. The room was beautifully decorated with a king-size cherry-oak sleigh bed, with matching armoire, nightstands, mirror and dresser. Numerous paintings adorned the walls and several silk flower arrangements added a beautiful touch. It was basically a minisuite with a sitting area and large connecting bath.

"My mom fixed things up in here. She says the other guest rooms looked too manly for her."

Savannah turned and looked into Durango's eyes. Their gazes locked for the space of ten, maybe twelve heartbeats. "I like it and thank you. It's beautiful," she said, moments later breaking eye contact and glancing around the beautifully appointed room once again, attempting to get her control back intact.

Out of the corner of her eyes she saw him move closer into the room. She turned slightly and watched as he walked over to the window and pulled back the curtains. His concentration was on the view outside, but heaven help her, her concentration was on him. And what a view he was. How a man so tall, long-legged and muscular could move with such fluid grace was beyond her. But he managed to do so rather nicely.

She had noticed that about him from the first. There

was something inherently masculine about Durango Westmoreland and the single night they had made love, she had discovered that what you saw was what you got. He definitely could deliver. That night he had tilted her universe in such a way that she knew it would never be the same again. Even now, a warmth moved slowly through all parts of her body just thinking about all the things they had done that night. No second, minute or hour had been wasted.

Durango suddenly turned and his gaze rested on her, longer than she deemed necessary, before he said, "It looks simply beautiful out of this window. Nothing but mountains all around. And this time of year when the snow falls, I think it's the most gorgeous sight that you'd ever want to see." He then turned back around and looked out the window again.

Mildly interested and deciding not to pretend otherwise, Savannah crossed the room to stand beside him and her breath caught. He was absolutely right. The panoramic view outside the window was beautiful. She hoped she had the chance to capture a lot of it on film before she left. "Have you lived here long?" curiosity pushed her to ask.

He met her gaze and smiled. "Almost five years now. After I finished college and got a job with the park ranger service, I lived with my uncle Corey on his mountain for a couple of years, until I saved enough money to buy this land. It was originally part of a homestead, but after the elderly couple who owned it passed on, their offspring split up the property and put individual parcels up for sale. My ranch sits on over a hundred acres."

"Wow! That's a lot of land."

He smiled. "Yes, but most of it is mountains, which is one of the things that drew me to it. And a good portion of it is a natural hot springs. The first thing I did after building the ranch house was to erect my own private hot tub out back. If the weather wasn't so bad, I'd let you try it out. A good soak it in would definitely guarantee you a good night's sleep."

Savannah couldn't help but smile at the thought of that. "A good night's sleep sounds wonderful. The flight out here was awful."

Durango chuckled. "Unfortunately it usually is." He then checked his watch. "How about I put dinner on the table? Earlier I smothered pieces of chicken in gravy, and made cabbage and mashed potatoes. You're welcome to join me after you settle in."

Savannah felt her stomach growl at the mention of food. Dinner was her favorite mealtime since she could never keep any breakfast down for too long. The only thing she had risked eating that day had been saltines. "Thanks, and I'd like that. Do you need any help?"

"No, I have everything under control." He turned to leave the room then stopped before walking out the door. "You're a city girl, but your name isn't."

Savannah arched a brow. She remembered what Jessica had shared with her once regarding Durango's aversion to city women. "It's my mom's favorite Southern city and she thought the name suited me."

He nodded, thinking the name suited her very feminine and genteel charm, as well.

A short while later Savannah followed the aroma of food as she walked down the stairs to the kitchen. She stopped and glanced around, getting a good look at the wood-grain kitchen counters and the shiny stainless-steel appliances. The kitchen was a cook's dream. From one side of the ceiling hung an assortment of copper pots. Unlike most men, Durango evidently enjoyed spending time in his kitchen.

He must have heard her sigh of admiration because he then turned, looked at her and smiled. "All settled in?"

Forcing her nervousness away, she nodded. "Yes. I didn't bring much since I hadn't planned on staying."

"You might as well get comfortable. I wouldn't be surprised if you're stuck here for a couple of days."

Savannah frowned. "Why would you think that?"

Durango leaned back against the counter and gestured toward the window. "Take a look outside."

Savannah walked quickly over to the window. There was a full-scale blizzard going on. She could barely see anything. She turned around. "What happened?"

Durango chuckled. "Welcome to Montana. Didn't you know this was the worst time of year to come visiting?"

No, she hadn't known. The only thing that had been on her mind, once she'd made her decision, was to get to him and tell him about the baby as soon as she could.

She glanced back out the window. "And you think this will last a couple of days?"

"More than likely. The only thing we can do is to make the most of it."

Savannah turned and met his gaze, taking in what he'd just said. It was simply a play on words, she presumed. She hoped. Being cooped up in the house with Durango for a couple of days and *making the most of it* wasn't what she'd planned on happening. It didn't take much to recall just how quickly she had succumbed to his sexiness. All it had taken was a little eye contact and she'd been a goner.

"Come on, Savannah. Let's eat."

Savannah regarded him for a moment before crossing the room to the table where he'd placed the food. "Aren't you concerned about losing power?"

Durango shook his head. "Nope. I have my own generator. It's capable of supplying all the energy I need to keep this place running awhile. Then there are the fireplaces. I had one built for every bedroom as well as the living room. No matter how cold or nasty the weather gets outside, you can believe we'll stay warm and cozy inside."

Staying warm and cozy was another thing she was afraid of, Savannah thought, taking a seat at the table. There was no doubt in her mind that she and Durango could supply enough sensuous fire to actually torch the place.

"Everything looks delicious. I didn't know you could cook," she said, helping herself to some of the food he had prepared, and trying not to lick her lips in the process. She was so hungry.

Durango smiled as he watched her dig in, glad she had a good appetite. A lot of the women he'd dated acted as if it was a sin to eat more than a thimbleful of food. "I'm a bachelor who believes in knowing how to fend for myself. On top of that I'm Sarah Westmoreland's son. She taught me Survival 101 well."

Savannah tasted the mashed potatoes and thought they were delicious. "Mmm, these are good."

"Thanks."

After a few moments of silence Durango said, "I noticed you aren't showing yet."

Savannah met his eyes. She had felt the heat of his gaze on her, checking out her body, when she'd crossed the room to stand at the window. "I'm only two months, Durango. The baby is probably smaller than a peanut now. Most women don't start showing until their fourth month."

He nodded. "How has the pregnancy been for you so far?"

She shrugged. "The usual, I guess. What I'm battling now more than anything is the morning sickness. Usually I don't dare eat anything but saltines before two o'clock every day, which is why I'm so hungry now."

Durango's eyes widened. "You're sick every day?"

He looked so darn surprised at the thought of such a thing that she couldn't help but chuckle. "Yes, just about. But according to the doctor, it will only last for another month or so."

She tilted her head and looked at him. "Haven't you ever been around a pregnant woman?"

"No, not for any length of time. When I went home for Easter last year, Jayla was pregnant and boy, was she huge. Of course, she was having twins." He grinned. "Twins run in my family and there's even a set of triplets."

Savannah raised her eyes heavenward. "Thanks for telling me."

Catching her off guard, Durango reached across the table and captured a lock of her hair in his hand, gently twining the soft, silky strands in his fingers. "I think triplets would be nice, and all with beautiful hazel eyes like yours."

Savannah swallowed tightly as her grip on sanity

weakened. The way he was looking at her wasn't helping matters. She sensed his intense reaction to her was just as potent as hers to him. It was just as strong as it had been that night, and at that moment the desire to have his hands on her again, touching her breasts, her thighs, the area between her legs, was strong and unexpected. If he were to try anything right now, anything at all, it would take all her willpower to resist him.

"I want to be around and see how your body changes with my baby growing inside you, Savannah," he whispered huskily.

His words flowed over Savannah, caressing her in places she didn't want to be touched, and making a slow ache seep through her bones. "I don't know how that will be possible, Durango," she whispered softly.

"It would be possible if we got married."

She frowned and pulled back from him, breaking their contact. "You agreed not to bring that up again."

A smile touched the corners of his lips. "I know, but I want to make you an offer that I hope you can't refuse."

She lifted her eyebrows. "What kind of offer?"

"That we marry and set a limit on the amount of time we'll stay together. We could remain married during the entire length of your pregnancy and for a short while afterward—say six to nine months. After that, we could file for a divorce."

She was stunned by his proposal. "What would doing something like that accomplish?" she asked, feeling the weight of his gaze on her and wishing she could ignore it.

"First, it would satisfy my need and desire to be with you during your pregnancy. Second, it would eliminate the stigma of my child being born illegitimate, which is something that is unacceptable to me. And third, because you believe I'll end up doing to you what your father did to your mother, at least this way you'll know up front that the marriage will be short-term and you won't lose any sleepless nights."

Savannah's frown deepened. "I never said I thought you would do me the way my father did my mother."

"Not in so many words, but it's clear you believe if I married you just for the baby that things wouldn't work out between us. And in a way I have to agree. You're probably right. Our marriage would be based on a sense of obligation on my part. There has to be more to hold a marriage together than just a baby. And to be quite honest with you, I'm not looking for a long-term marriage. But a short-term union, for our baby's sake, would be acceptable to me. I believe it would be acceptable to you, as well, because we'd know what to expect and not to expect from the relationship."

It seemed like a million questions were flashing in Savannah's mind, but she knew the main one that she needed to ask. "Are you saying you'd want a marriage in name only? A marriage of convenience?"

"Yes."

She swallowed and continued to meet his gaze. "And that means we won't be sharing a bed?"

He studied her for a moment and knew what she was getting at. His desire for her was as natural as it could get, and he didn't see it lessening any. If he wanted her at such a high degree now, he could just imagine how things would be once they were living together as man and wife under the same roof. Yes, he would definitely want to sleep with her.

Leaning back in his chair, he said, "No, not exactly. I have other ideas on the matter."

She could just imagine those ideas. "Then keep whatever ideas you have to yourself. *If,* and I said *if,* I go along with what you're proposing, we will *not* share a bed."

"Are you saying that you didn't enjoy sleeping with me?"

Savannah huffed an agitated sigh. Who had slept that night? Neither of them had until the wee hours of the morning. From what she remembered—and she was remembering it quite well—it was round-the-clock sex. And she had to admit, it was the best she'd ever had. The year she'd spent with Thomas couldn't even compare. "That's not the point."

"Then what *is* the point?" Durango countered.

"The point is," Savannah said, narrowing her eyes at him, "regardless of the fact that I did sleep with you that night, I usually don't jump into any man's bed unless I'm serious about him." She decided not to tell him that she'd only been serious with two other guys in her entire love-life history.

He leaned forward. "Trust me, Savannah, once we're married, we'll be as serious as any couple can get, even if we plan for our marriage to last a short while. Frankly I see no reason why we shouldn't sleep together. We're adults with basic needs who know what we want, and I think we need to start being honest with ourselves. We're attracted to each other, and have been from the first, which is why we're in this predicament. Things got as hot as it gets.

"And," he continued with an impatient wave of his

hand to stop her from saying whatever it was that she was about to say, "we might not have been in our right minds that night, since we might have overindulged in the champagne, but we did enjoy making love. So why pretend otherwise?"

Savannah scowled. She wasn't pretending; she just didn't want a repeat performance, regardless of how enjoyable it had been. "You're missing the point."

"No, I think that you are. You're pregnant and I want to be a part of this pregnancy. It's important that I be there with you during the time you're carrying our baby, to bond with him or her while he or she's still in your womb and for some months following that."

"And just how long are you talking about?"

"Whatever period of time we agree on, but I prefer nothing less than six months. I'd even go into another year if I had to."

She frowned. "I wouldn't want you to do me any favors."

"It's not about doing you any favors, Savannah. I intend to always be a part of my child's life regardless of whether you and I are together. But I think six months afterward should be sufficient, unless you want longer."

When hell freezes over. For a few moments Savannah didn't say anything. What could she say when he was right? They had been attracted to each other from the first.

But what happened that night was in the past and she refused to willingly tumble back into bed with him again, and he had another thought coming if he assumed that she would. Evidently he was used to getting what he wanted, but in this case he wouldn't be so lucky.

She then thought about the other thing he'd said, about wanting to connect to their child while it was still in her womb. She remembered reading in one of her baby books how such a thing was possible and important to the baby's well-being. Some couples even played music and read books to their child while it was still growing inside the mother. Never in her wildest dreams would she have thought that Durango would know, much less care, about such things.

She pushed her plate back, glad she had eaten everything since it would probably be the last meal she'd be able to consume until this time tomorrow. "I need to think about what you're suggesting, Durango."

At the lift of his brow she decided to clarify. "I'm talking about the marriage of convenience *without* you having any bedroom rights. If your offer hinges on the opposite then there's nothing for me to think about. I won't be sleeping with you, marriage or no marriage." She then thought of something.

"And where would we live if I went along with what you're proposing?" she asked.

He shrugged broad shoulders. "I prefer here, but if you want I can move to Philly."

Savannah knew that Durango was a man of the mountains. Here he was in his element and she couldn't imagine him living in Philadelphia of all places. "What about your job?"

"I'll take a leave."

She lifted an eyebrow. "You'd be willing to do that?"

"For our child, yes."

She searched his face and saw the sincerity in his words, and they overwhelmed her as well as frightened her. He was letting her know up front that although he didn't want a long-term commitment, he was willing to engage in a short-term one for the sake of her child.

Their child.

She stood. "Like I said, I need to think about this, Durango."

"And I want you to think about it and think about it good. If you're dead set against us sharing a bed then that's fine. My offer of marriage still stands."

He stood and came around the table to stand in front of her. "There are bath towels, a robe and whatever else you might need in the private bath adjoining your room. If you need anything else let me know. Otherwise, I'll see you in the morning."

"I'll help you with the dishes and—"

"No, leave them," he said quickly, releasing a frustrated breath. There was only so much temptation that he could handle and at that moment he wanted nothing more than to kiss her, taste her. But he knew that now was not the time. She needed a chance to think about his offer.

"I'll take care of the dishes later after checking out a few things around my property," he added.

"You sure?"

"Yes."

"All right."

Durango watched as Savannah quickly walked off. He couldn't help but shake his head. Nothing had changed. The attraction between them was still as hot as it got.

Four

The next morning Savannah awoke more confused than ever. She had barely gotten any sleep for thinking about Durango's proposal. In a way it could make their mistake even bigger. On the other hand, he seemed sincere in wanting to help her through her pregnancy, and she wouldn't deny him the chance to bond with his child, especially when very few men would care to do so.

Deciding she didn't want to think about Durango's proposal any longer, she sat up in bed and glanced out the window. The weather was worse than it had been the day before, which meant she couldn't leave today unless the conditions miraculously cleared up.

At least the fireplace was blazing, providing warmth to the room. She settled back in bed, and remembered opening her eyes some point during the night and seeing Durango in front of the fireplace, squatting on his heels and leaning forward, trying to get the fire going. At the time she had been too tired and sleepy to acknowledge his presence.

With the aid of the moon's glow streaming through the window, she had lain there and watched him. A different kind of heat had engulfed her as she watched him working to bring warmth to the room. His shirt had stretched tight to accommodate broad shoulders and the hands that had held the wrought-iron poker had been strong and capable...just as they'd been the night he had used them on her. And later, when he had pushed himself to his feet, she had admired his physique—especially his backside—through heavy-lidded eyes, thinking that he had the best-looking butt to ever grace a pair of jeans.

She startled when there was a knock on her door. Knowing it could only be Durango, she swallowed hard and said, "Come in."

He walked in, bringing enough heat into the room to make the fireplace unnecessary, and his smile made Savannah's insides curl, making her feel even hotter there. How would she ever be able to remain immune to his lethal charm?

"Good morning, Savannah. I hope you rested well."

"Good morning, Durango, and I did. Thanks. I see the weather hasn't improved," she said, sitting up in bed and tucking the covers modestly around her chest. Because she hadn't figured this would be an extended trip, besides her camera pack, which she was rarely without, she'd only brought a book to read on the plane, her makeup and one change of clothing. She'd been forced to sleep in an oversize Atlanta Braves T-shirt that she had found in one of the dresser drawers.

"No, the weather has gotten worse and I need to leave for a while and—"

"You're going out in that?" she asked.

His eyebrows raised a half inch and the smile on his face deepened. "This is nothing compared to a storm that blew through last month. I'm a member of the Search and Rescue Squad so I'm used to going out and working in these conditions. I just got a call from the station. A couple of hikers are missing so we have to go out and find them. There're a number of isolated cabins around these parts and I'm hoping they sought shelter in one of them."

She nodded and moved her gaze from his to glance out the window again. She couldn't imagine anyone being caught out in the weather and hoped the hikers were safe.

"Will you be all right until I get back?" he asked.

She met his gaze again. "I'll be fine." She watched as he turned to leave and quickly said, "Be careful."

Pausing to glance back at her, he said, "I will." He smiled again and added, "I don't intend for you to give birth to our child without me."

Savannah had hoped this morning would be different, but as soon as her feet touched the floor she began experiencing her usual bout of morning sickness and quickly rushed to the bathroom.

A short while later, after brushing her teeth, rinsing out her mouth and soaking her body in a hot tub of water, she wrapped herself in a thick white velour robe that was hanging in the closet and padded barefoot to the kitchen, hoping Durango kept saltine crackers on hand.

A sigh of gratitude escaped her lips when she found a box in his pantry and opened the pack and began consuming a few to settle her stomach. She walked over to the window and glanced out at the abundance of twirling snowflakes. If it kept snowing at this rate there was no telling when she would get a flight out.

Durango stomped the snow off his shoes before stepping inside his home. The thought of Savannah being there when he returned was what had gotten him through the blinding cold while the search party had looked for the hikers. Luckily they had found them in fairly good condition in an old, abandoned cabin.

Quietly closing the door behind him, he slid out of his coat and glanced across the room. Savannah was curled up on the sofa, asleep. Her dark, curly hair framed her face, making her even more beautiful. She looked so peaceful, as if she didn't have a care in the world, and he could have stood there indefinitely and watched her sleep.

When she stirred slightly it hit him that even now something was taking place inside her body. His seed had taken root and was forming, shaping and growing into another human being. For a brief moment a smile touched his lips as he envisioned a little girl with her mother's black curly locks, caramel-colored skin and beautiful hazel eyes.

Females born into the Westmoreland family had been a rarity and for almost thirty years his cousin Delaney had been the only one, having the unenviable task of trying to handle a dozen very protective Westmorelands—her father, five brothers and six male cousins.

Then, just eighteen months ago, it was discovered that his uncle Corey had fathered triplets that included a girl—Casey. Mercifully, this discovery had taken some of the attention off Delaney.

Now Storm and Jayla had daughters and he heard that Dare and Shelly, as well as Delaney and Jamal, who had sons already, were hoping for girls this time around. Just the thought of a future generation of female Westmorelands made him shudder. But still, he liked the idea of having a daughter to pamper, a daughter who was a miniature version of Savannah.

He had to admit there were a number of things about the woman asleep on his couch that stirred feelings inside him. One was the fact that she hadn't used her pregnancy to force his hand. He could name a number of women who definitely would have shown up demanding that they marry by the end of the day. Savannah, on the other hand, hadn't been thrilled by the suggestion and even now hadn't agreed to go along with him on it. For some reason Durango liked the thought of having her tied to him legally, even for a short while.

He gazed down at her. She was wearing the oversize T-shirt and jogging pants that he had left out for her. Both were his and fit rather large on her. Even so, he couldn't help but notice the curve of her breasts beneath the cotton shirt. They seemed larger than he'd remembered. It was going to be interesting, as well as fascinating, to watch her body go through the changes it would endure during the coming months. And more than anything, he wanted to be around to see it.

He shook his head, thinking that if anyone had told him last week he would be feeling this way about a pregnant woman, he would not have believed them. He knew he would have a hard time convincing his best friend, McKinnon Quinn, that he'd not only accepted Savannah's pregnancy but was looking forward to the day she gave birth. He and McKinnon were known to be the die-hard bachelors around these parts and had always made it a point to steer clear of any type of binding relationship.

When Savannah made a soft, nearly soundless sigh in her sleep and shifted her body, making the T-shirt rise a little to uncover her stomach, Durango stifled a groan and was tempted to go over and kiss the part of her body where his child was nestled. He closed his eyes as his imagination took over when he knew he wouldn't want to stop at just her stomach. Even now her seductive scent filled the room and tantalized his senses. He felt tired, exhausted, yet at the same time he felt his body stirring when he remembered the heated passion the two of them had once shared. A passion he was looking forward to them sharing again one day.

Savannah awoke with a start, immediately aware that she was no longer alone. The smell of food cooking was a dead giveaway.

Her memory returned in a rush and she recalled her bout with morning sickness and how she had decided to lie on the sofa when a moment of dizziness had assailed her. She must have fallen asleep. She couldn't help wondering when Durango had returned. Why hadn't he awakened her? Had they found the missing hikers?

"Did you eat anything?"

The sound of Durango's deep voice nearly made her jump. She met his gaze and instantly, her body was filled with a deep, throbbing heat. He had removed the pullover sweater he'd been wearing over his jeans earlier and was dressed in a casual shirt that was open at the throat, giving him a downright sexy appeal, not that he needed it.

There was something about him that just turned her on. It would be hard to be married to him—even on a short-term basis—without there ever being a chance of them sharing a bed. But she was determined to do just that.

Knowing she hadn't answered him, she said, "No, but thanks for leaving breakfast warming for me in the oven. My stomach wasn't cooperating and I wouldn't have been able to keep anything down. I found some saltines in your pantry and decided to munch on those."

Durango nodded, recalling her mentioning the previous day that she'd been unable to eat most mornings. "Have you seen a doctor?"

"Yes, although I'm going to have to find another one soon. Dr. Wilson is the same doctor who delivered me and Rico and he's retiring next month."

"Isn't he concerned with you being sick every day? Are you and the baby getting all the nutrients you need?"

Savannah shrugged as she sat up. "Healthwise Dr. Wilson says that both the baby and I are fine."

He leaned back against the wall. "When you go to the doctor again I'd like to be there."

"In Philadelphia?"

"Wherever you decide to go doesn't matter. And since your doctor is retiring, just so you'll know, there's a good obstetrician here in Bozeman and she's female."

She tipped her head back and looked at him and wished she could stop her pulse from racing at the sight of his lean, hard body. "Really? That's good to know."

He smiled. "I thought it would be."

He came into the room and sat in the chair across from her, stretching his long legs out and crossing them at a booted ankle. "Have you thought about what I proposed last night?"

"Yes, I thought about it."

"And?" he asked gently, knowing she was a woman who couldn't be rushed.

"And I need more time to make up my mind," she said, fixing her gaze on his boots.

"I wish I could tell you to take all the time you need, but time isn't on our side, Savannah. If we do decide to get married there needs to be a wedding."

Her head snapped up. "A wedding?"

He smiled at her surprised expression. "Yes. I don't anticipate one as elaborate as Chase's, but as you know, we Westmorelands are a large family with plenty of friends and acquaintances and—"

"It's not as if it would be a real marriage, Durango, so why bother?"

"Because my parents, specifically my mother, who won't know why we're getting married, would expect it."

"Well, personally I can't see the need for a lot of hoopla over something that won't last. If I decide to accept your proposal, I prefer that we go off somewhere like Vegas and not tell anyone about it until it's over. They will eventually know the real reason we got married in a few months anyway."

Durango nodded, knowing she was right. His family,

who knew how he felt about marriage, would know it wasn't the real thing no matter what he told them. "What about your mother?"

"She's leaving tomorrow for Paris and won't be back for a couple of weeks. If I do decide to marry you, she'll be okay with my decision and it won't bother me that she won't be at the ceremony since she knows I don't believe in happily-ever-after."

Durango rubbed the back of his neck with an irritated frown. It wasn't that he didn't believe in fairy-tale romances, but after Tricia he figured it would be more fantasy than reality for him. "Fine. If you agree, we can elope and then if our parents want to do something in the way of a reception later, that will be fine. All right?"

She sighed. "All right."

"So when will you let me know your decision?"

"Before I leave here. Do you think the weather will have improved by tomorrow?"

"I'm not sure. Usually these types of snowstorms can last for a week."

"A week? I didn't bring enough clothes with me."

He thought now was not a good time to tell her he wouldn't mind if she walked around naked. "The last time Delaney was here she left a few of her things behind. The two of you are around the same size so you should be able to fit into them if you want to try."

"You don't think she'd mind?"

"No."

"All right then, if you're sure it's okay."

He stood. "Do you think your stomach has settled enough for dinner? I cooked a pot of beef stew."

"Yes, I think it will be able to handle it. Would you like some help in the kitchen?"

"If you're up to it you can set the table."

She stood. "I'm up to it. Did you find the hikers?"

"Yes, we found them and they're fine. Luckily one was a former Boy Scout and knew exactly what to do."

She smiled, relieved, as she followed him into the kitchen. "I'm glad."

Savannah was amazed at the degree of her appetite and flushed with embarrassment when she noted that Durango had stopped to watch her, with amusement dancing in his eyes, as she devoured one bowl of stew and was working on her second.

She licked her lips. "I was hungry."

"Apparently."

When she pushed the empty bowl aside, he chuckled and said, "Hey, you were on a roll. Don't stop on my account."

Her brows came together in a frown. "I've had enough, thank you."

"You're welcome. I've got to keep the ballerina on her toes."

"What ballerina?"

"Our daughter."

Savannah raised a glass of milk to her lips, took a sip and then asked, "You think I'm having a girl?"

"Yes."

She tipped her head, curious. "Why?"

He leaned forward to wipe the milk from around her lips with his napkin, wondering when the last time he had given so much time and attention to a woman was.

"Because that's what I want and I'm arrogant enough to think I'll get whatever I want."

Savannah didn't doubt that—not that she thought he got anything and everything he wanted, but that he was arrogant enough to think so. "Why would you want a girl?"

"Why wouldn't I want one?" he asked. There was no way he would tell her the reason he wanted a little girl was that he wanted a daughter who looked just like her. He couldn't explain the reasoning behind it and at the moment he didn't want to dwell on the significance of it.

"There are more males in your family, and considering that, I'd think for you a son would be easier to manage," she said.

He chuckled, amused. "I think we managed my cousin Delaney just fine. With five brothers and six older male cousins we were able to put the fear of God into any guy who showed interest in her. I see no problem with us getting the same point across with the next generation of Westmoreland females."

His smile deepened. "Besides, don't you know that girls are the apples of their fathers' eyes?"

"Not in all cases," she said, thinking of the relationship she and Jessica never had with their father.

"But let me set the record straight," Durango said, breaking into her reverie. "I would love either a boy or girl, but having a daughter would be extra, extra special."

Savannah smiled, thinking his words pleased her, probably because she was hoping for a girl, as well. In some ways it surprised her that a man who was such a confirmed bachelor would want children or be interested in fatherhood at all.

At that moment an adorable image floated into her mind of Durango and a little girl who looked just like him sitting on his lap while he read her a story.

"So what do you think?" Durango asked.

Savannah glanced up after going through the items of clothing that Durango had placed on the bed. "I think they'll work. I don't wear jeans often so the change will be nice, and the sweaters look comfy. They will be good for this weather."

"So what do you plan to do tonight?"

The low-pitch murmur of his voice had her lifting her head and meeting his gaze. She wished there was some way she didn't get turned on whenever she looked into their dark depths. "I thought I'd try and finish a book that I brought with me."

"Oh, and what type book is it?"

She shrugged. "One of those baby books that tells you what to expect during pregnancy and at childbirth."

"Sounds interesting."

"It is." She tried ignoring the sensations that were moving around in her stomach. Having Durango in her bedroom wasn't a good idea and the sooner she got him out, the better, but there was something that she needed to find out first.

"There's something I'd like to ask you, Durango. It's something I need to know before I can make a decision about marrying you."

He lifted an eyebrow. "And what is it you need to know?"

She moved away from the bed and sank down on the love seat. She would have preferred having any conversation with him someplace else other than here, in the coziness of the bedroom with a fireplace burning with its yellow glow illuminating Durango's handsome features even more. At least she wasn't standing next to the bed any longer.

Knowing he was waiting for her to speak, she met his gaze and asked, "I want to know what you have against *city women*."

Five

Some questions weren't meant to be asked.

Savannah quickly reached that conclusion when she saw Durango's jaw clench, his hands tighten into a fist by his side and an angry flare darken his eyes. Another thing that was a dead giveaway was the sudden chill in the air, not to mention the force of his stare, which caused her to draw a quick breath.

Her question, which had evidently caught him off guard, was calling for every bit of his self-control and she began feeling uneasy. Still, she needed to know the reason for his aversion since it was something that obviously quite a few people knew, at least those who were close to him.

She watched his lips move and knew he was muttering something under his breath. That only increased her curiosity, her need to know. "Durango?"

When he finally spoke his voice was low with an edginess that hinted she had waded into forbidden waters. "I'd rather not talk about it."

Savannah knew she should probably let the matter drop, but she couldn't let the question die because a part of her really wanted to know.

Evidently he saw that determined look in her features and he said, "It doesn't concern you, Savannah. You're having my baby. I've asked you to marry me so there's no need for us to start spilling our guts on every little thing that happened in our pasts. I'll respect your right to privacy and I hope that you will respect mine."

Savannah couldn't help wondering about what he didn't want to tell her. What pain was he still hiding in his heart? God knew she had plenty of skeletons she'd kept hidden in her mental closet. Secrets she'd only shared with Jessica. His request for privacy was a reasonable one. She shouldn't be digging into his past, but she needed assurance that whatever his problem was, she wouldn't be affected by it, and until she had that certainty, she wouldn't back off.

"All that's well and good, Durango, but if I am to marry you, even if it's only for a short while, I need to know I won't be mistreated because of someone else's transgressions."

"You won't."

The words had been spoken so quickly that Savannah hadn't had a chance to blink. She heard both regret and anger in his voice.

"This is only about you and me, Savannah, and no one else. Don't let anything that happened before sway your decision now."

Savannah's gaze wandered over his muscular form. He was leaning with a shoulder pressed up against a bedpost, his booted feet crossed at the ankles and his arms folded over his chest. He was watching her with as much intensity as she was watching him.

Seconds ticked by and with the passing of time something heated and all-consuming was passing between them. And she knew if it continued that she couldn't be responsible for her actions…and neither could he.

Even now he was spiking heat inside her just standing there, saying nothing. She continued to feel an overpowering need. Desire was inching its way up her spine and then she remembered his taste and how she couldn't get enough of him the last time.

He continued to hold her gaze and he was having a hypnotic effect on her. And then he moved toward her, with his slow, graceful stride. Crossing the room, he reached out and gently tugged her up off the sofa.

She knew at that moment what he wanted, what he needed. They were the same things she desired. Lowering his face, bending to cup the back of her head with his hand, he kissed her. The moment their lips touched, her hands automatically slipped inside the back pockets of his jeans. It was that or remain free and be tempted to squeeze his butt like Mr. Whipple used to squeeze the Charmin.

And when their lips locked and he inserted his tongue inside her mouth, the contact was so intimate, heated and passionate that she knew there was nothing she could do but stand there and enjoy it.

And she did.

They were consenting adults and a little kiss never

hurt anyone, she convinced herself when her tongue joined in with his. But this was no little kiss, she discovered moments later. The tongue stroking hers was strong and capable, arousing her to a pitch higher than he'd done that night in her hotel room.

It was the usual Durango kiss—long, hot, sexy. The kind of kiss that made your toes curl, your breasts feel full and your stomach tingle. She closed her eyes to feel more deeply the sensations that crowded her mind and the electrical charges that were burning all over her body. She breathed in his scent, glorying in the slow, methodical way he was making love to her mouth.

Too soon, he reluctantly broke off the kiss. She slowly opened her eyes, met the deep intensity of his gaze, expelled a deep breath, then dragged in an unsteady one, feeling satisfied. And even now she saw his gaze was still locked on to her lips.

"I enjoy kissing you," he said softly, throatily, as if that explained everything, especially every tantalizing stroke of his tongue.

She watched those dark, intense eyes that were focused on her mouth get even darker. "Um, I can tell."

She had to admit that nothing about her visit to his home had turned out like she'd planned. She had come to tell her news and leave. It was too bad she hadn't stuck to her plans. But then, if she had, she wouldn't be standing here discovering once again what true passion was like. Before meeting him, she hadn't had a clue.

"I think I'd better go. I'll see you in the morning," he whispered low against her moist lips.

And before she could blink or catch her next breath, he was gone.

* * *

The moment the door closed behind Durango, Savannah could feel her stomach muscles tightening. She swayed slightly when the floor beneath her feet felt shaky. Talk about a kiss!

Muttering darkly—probably some of those same words Durango had said earlier, but hadn't wanted her to hear—she crossed the room and dropped down on the bed. His kiss was one of the reasons she was in this predicament. She had invited him into her room for the two of them to indulge in some more champagne. She hadn't gotten to completely filling his glass before he had taken both the bottle and glass from her hand and had filled her mouth with his instead. He hadn't kissed her silly—he had kissed her crazy. The taste of him had been hot, delicious and incredibly pleasurable. She had lusted for him, after him, with him and by the time they had made it to the bed, they had stripped naked.

They were extremely attracted to each other. Deep down inside she knew that Durango didn't like their explosive chemistry any more than she did. She had seen the way his eyes had flashed when he had lifted his mouth from hers, as well as the way his jaw muscles had tightened. Also, there was the way he always looked after kissing her senseless, like he needed divine intervention to help him deal with her and the sexual response they stirred up in each other.

"And to think that he's proposing marriage," she mumbled in a low voice that rattled with frustration. "So okay, it will only be for a short while, as he's quick to remind me every chance he gets," she said, shifting to her back and folding her arms over her chest. "What will I get out of this arrangement?"

More kisses, her mind immediately responded. *And if you stop being so dang stubborn, you'd also get a temporary bed partner. What do you have to lose? You'll be entering into a relationship with your eyes open and no expectations. You'll know up front that love has nothing to do with it. Besides, you'll be giving your child a chance to develop a relationship with a father who cares.*

Because of her experience with her father, that meant everything to Savannah. She believed that even when their marriage ended, Durango would remain a major part of his child's life.

Savannah also needed to think about the other reasons why marrying Durango was a good idea.

Pulling her body up, she shifted to her side. First was the issue of having a temporary bed partner if she decided to go that route. She'd dated but had never been into casual sex so she hadn't been involved with anyone since Thomas Crawford. She had dated Thomas exclusively for a year and things between them had been going well until he'd gotten jealous about an assignment she'd gotten that he had wanted. He'd even tried convincing her to turn the job down so he could have it— talk about someone being selfish and self-centered. It had been over a year, close to two since she'd broken up with Thomas or slept with anyone. The night she had shared a bed with Durango hadn't just been a night of want for her; it had been a night of need, a strictly hormonal affair in which she really hadn't acted like herself.

She tipped her head to the side and moved on to the

other reason for marrying Durango. *Expectations.* Their expectations would be set and neither of them would be wearing blinders. She knew their marriage would not be the real thing. He didn't love her and she didn't love him. Having reasonable expectations would definitely make things easier emotionally when the time came for them to split.

The more she thought about it, the more she knew that accepting his offer of marriage was the best thing. Her child would be getting the type of father that she never had; a father her baby would be able to depend on.

And then there were all the other Westmorelands who would be her child's extended family. She had seen firsthand at Chase and Jessica's wedding just what a close-knit group they were. Being part of a large family was another thing she'd missed growing up, but it was something her child could have.

Her brain began spinning with all the positives, but she forced herself to think about the negatives, as well. At the moment she could only imagine one. *The possibility of her falling in love with him.*

She couldn't even envision such a thing happening, but she knew there was that possibility. Durango would not be a hard man to love. A woman could definitely lose her heart to him if she wasn't careful. He was so strong and assertive and yet, he was also a giving and a caring person. She noticed his sensitivity in the ways that he saw to her needs: making sure he'd left breakfast for her; coming into her room in the dead of night to make sure she was warm enough; inquiring about her and their baby's health.

But still, there was no way she could ever fall in

love. She doubted that she could give him or any man a slice of her soul or a piece of her heart.

She knew that no matter how much she enjoyed the time she would spend with Durango during her pregnancy, she could not lose her heart to him. Ever.

Several hours had passed since Durango and Savannah had shared that heated kiss, and the residual effects were so strong that he couldn't think straight enough to balance his accounting records. Instead of concentrating on debits and credits he was way too focused on the incredible sensations he was still feeling, the electrical jolts that were still flowing through his body.

He had kissed women, plenty of times, but none had left a mark on him like Savannah Claiborne had. There was something about her taste, a succulent blend of sweetness, innocence and lusciousness, all rolled into one tangy, overpowering flavor that sent all kinds of crazy, out-of-control feelings slithering all through his body. She made his temperature rise, clogged his senses and forced his pulse to race.

"Dammit."

He slapped the accounting books shut and turned away from the computer screen. The last thing he needed was to make a miscalculation on the ledger for the horse-breeding business he co-owned with his good friend McKinnon Quinn.

He leaned back in his chair and his thoughts returned to Savannah. He just hoped her decision would be the one he wanted. He simply refused to consider any other possibility.

Six

"What the hell! Savannah? Are you all right?"

Savannah heard the footsteps behind her. She also heard the concern as well as the panic in Durango's voice, but she was too weak to lift her head and turn around. She didn't want him to see her like this. How humiliating was it to be on your knees on the floor of a bathroom, holding your head over a commode?

"Savannah, what's wrong?"

The moment she could, she expelled a breath and said the two words she hoped would explain everything. It appeared that he hadn't gotten the picture yet. "Morning sickness."

"Morning sickness? Is this what morning sickness is all about?"

Savannah suppressed a groan. What had he thought it was about? She was about to give him a snappy answer when her stomach clenched warningly. It was just as well since at that moment her body quickly reminded her of her condition and without any control, she closed her eyes, lowered her head and continued to bring up portions of yesterday's dinner.

"What can I do?"

It was on the tip of her tongue to tell him what he could do was go away. She didn't need an audience. "Nothing," she managed to say moments later. "Please, just leave me alone."

"Not even if your life depended on it, sweetheart," he said softly. Crouching down on the floor beside her, he wrapped his arms gently around her and whispered, "We're in this thing together, remember? Let me help you."

Before she could tell him that she didn't need his help and there wasn't anything he could do, he proved her wrong when she felt another spasm of nausea. He took a damp washcloth and began tenderly wiping her face and mouth.

Then he held her while her stomach began settling down. She was so touched by this generous display of caring, she leaned against his supporting body, while his huge hand gently stroked her belly into calmness. And as if with a will of its own, her head fell within the curve of his shoulder. No man had ever shown her so much tenderness. Okay, she confessed silently, Rico had always been there for her when she needed him, but since he was her brother he didn't count.

"That's right, baby, just relax for a moment. Everything is going to be fine. I'm going to take care of you," he murmured softly, brushing his lips against her temple and placing a kiss on her forehead.

Then she heard the toilet flushing at the same time as she was scooped up in Durango's strong arms. And after closing down the toilet lid, he sat down on it with her cradled in his arms as he continued to gently stroke her stomach. A short while later, as if she weighed nothing, he stood and sat her on the countertop next to the sink.

"Do you think a soda will help settle your stomach?" he asked, staring down in her eyes.

With the intensity of his gaze, her breath nearly got clogged in her throat but she managed to say, "Yes."

"Will you be okay while I go and get you one?"

"Yes, I'll be fine."

He nodded. "I'll be right back."

As soon as he left, Savannah inhaled a deep breath. As usual, her bout with nausea was going away just as quickly as it had come. Deciding to take advantage of the time Durango was gone, she gently lowered her body off the counter and immediately began brushing her teeth. She had just finished rinsing out her mouth when Durango returned.

"Here you go."

She took the cold can of ginger ale he offered and after quickly pulling the tab, she took a sip, immediately feeling better. After finishing the rest she lowered the can from her mouth, licked her lips and said, "Thanks, I needed that."

She quickly began studying the can. Durango was staring at her and she felt embarrassed. She knew she looked a mess. One of the things she had learned at the all-girl school her grandparents had sent her to was that a lady never showed signs of weakness in front of a man.

She'd also been taught that a man was not supposed to see a woman at her worst. Unfortunately some things couldn't be helped. Besides, it wasn't as if she had invited him to join her in the bathroom this morning. Why had he come, anyway?

As if reading her mind, he said, "I know you said you usually don't eat anything in the morning, but I was about to have breakfast and wanted to check to make sure you didn't want to join me."

"I would not have been able to eat anything."

"Yeah, I can see why. And you go through this every morning?" he asked, and once again she heard the deep concern in his voice.

"Yes, but it's not always this bad. I guess eating all that stew at dinner last night wasn't such a good idea."

"Evidently. What did your doctor say about it?"

She sighed deeply. "There's not a lot he could say, Durango. During the early months of pregnancy, morning sickness happens."

"That's not good enough."

She held up both hands to stop him. She knew he was about to urge her to see a local doctor. "Look, not now, okay? More than anything I need to get myself together. Just give me a few minutes."

"And you're sure you're okay?"

"I'm sure."

"Is there anything else I can get you?"

She shifted uneasily, not used to this amount of attention. "No, thanks. I don't need anything."

He nodded. "Okay then, I'll leave you alone to get dressed."

He turned to leave then slowly turned back around

and surprised her when his mouth brushed over hers. "Sorry my kid is causing you so much trouble," he said after the light caress.

And before she could gather her wits and say anything, he had walked out of the bathroom, leaving her alone.

Durango paced the living room, glad he hadn't gone out. He winced at the thought of how things would have been for Savannah if she'd been alone. Then it struck him that she *had* gone through it alone before. She lived by herself and there had to have been times when she'd been sick and no one had been there with her. When she'd first mentioned this morning sickness thing, he'd thought she just experienced a queasy stomach in the morning and preferred not eating until later. He had no idea she spent part of each morning practically retching her guts out.

He paused and rubbed his hand down his face. It was easy to see he wasn't used to being around a pregnant woman. There hadn't been any babies in his family until Delaney had given birth a few years ago, and then she'd spent most of the time during her pregnancy in her husband's homeland in the Middle East.

Although he had only been around Jayla a few times while she was pregnant, the only thing he'd been aware of was that she was huge. Because she had been carrying twins she always looked as if she was about to deliver at any moment. He didn't recall Storm ever mentioning anything about Jayla being sick and throwing up every morning. It seemed that he needed to be the one reading a baby book.

Shoving his hands into the pockets of his jeans, he

began pacing again. Okay, so maybe he was getting freaked out and carried away. Savannah had claimed what she was going through was normal, but even so, that didn't mean he had to like it.

He turned when he heard the sound of her entering the room. As he studied her he found it hard to believe she was the same woman who just moments ago had looked as if she were on the brink of death. Talk about a stunning transformation. She had changed into a pair of jeans and a top and both looked great on her. Immediately the thought came to his mind that she looked good in anything she put on her body, whether it was an expensive gown, slacks and a top, jeans or an oversize T-shirt.

She had added a touch of makeup to her features, but mainly her natural beauty was shining through, and it was shining so brightly that it made the room glow... which wasn't hard to do considering the weather outside. The storm was still at its worst, although the recent weather reports indicated things would start clearing up at some point that day.

"You okay?" he asked, quickly crossing the room to her.

She smiled faintly up at him. "Yes, I'm fine and I want to apologize for—"

"Don't. There's nothing to apologize for. I'm glad I was here."

She hated to admit it, but she was glad he'd been there, too. Although she had gone through the same ordeal alone countless times, it had felt good to have a shoulder to lean on. And it had been extremely nice knowing that that particular shoulder belonged to the man who had a vested interest in her condition.

She also didn't want to admit that she was fully aware of how handsome he looked this morning. Though to be honest, he always looked good in jeans and the Western shirts he liked to wear. Deciding she needed to think about other things, she walked over to the window and glanced out. She noticed the weather was still stormy. "Will you have to go out today?"

He moved to stand beside her and glanced out the window, as well. "Maybe later. The reports indicate the weather will begin clearing up soon."

"It will?" she asked, surprised, turning to face him.

"Yes."

She smiled brightly. "That means there's a possibility I'll be able to leave today."

"Yes, there is that possibility," he said. "I know you can't eat a heavy breakfast but is there something I can get for you that might agree with your stomach?"

"Um, a couple of saltines and a cup of herbal tea might work."

"Then saltines and herbal tea it is," he said, turning and walking toward the kitchen.

"And Durango?"

He turned back to her. "Yes?"

With her heart pounding she said, "I've made a decision about your proposal. I think we should talk about it."

He nodded. "All right. We can sit and talk at the kitchen table if you'd like."

"Okay," she said, and followed him into the kitchen.

"So, what have you decided?"

Savannah lifted her head from studying the saltines on the plate in front of her. She had thought things through most of the night but his actions that morning had only solidified her decision.

She set down her cup of tea and met his gaze. "I'm going to take you up on your offer and marry you."

She watched as he sat back in the chair and looked at her with something akin to relief. "But I'd like to explain the reasons for my decision and why I still won't sleep with you," she added.

"All right."

She paused after taking another sip of her tea, and then said, "I think I told you I didn't want to get married just because I was pregnant."

He nodded. "Because of that ordeal with your father, right?"

"Yes."

"How did your parents meet?"

"In college. When Mom showed up at her parents' house with my father over spring break in her senior year of college and announced that she planned to marry him after she graduated and that she was pregnant, my grandparents hit the roof. You see, my maternal grandparents never approved of interracial romances, so they weren't too happy about my parents' relationship."

"I can imagine they weren't."

"Those were certainly not the future plans that Roger and Melissa Billingslea had for their daughter. But nothing would change my mother's mind. She thought Jeff Claiborne was the best thing since raisin bread and when they couldn't convince her that he wasn't, my grandparents threatened to disown my mother."

"Did that work?"

"No. Mom and Dad were married a few months later.

According to Mom things were great at first, but then he lost his job with this big corporation and had to take a job as a traveling salesman. That's when things started going downhill. Dad began changing. However, it took almost fifteen years for her to find out that he'd been living a double life and that he had a mistress as well as another daughter living out west."

Durango took a sip of coffee. Chase had pretty much told him the story one night over a can of beer.

"It wasn't easy for me and Rico growing up," she said, reclaiming his attention. "Some people view children from mixed marriages as if they are from another planet. But with Mom's help we got past all of that, and eventually my grandparents came around. And it didn't take long for them to try to take over our lives. My grandmother even paid for me to go to an all-girl high school. But when it came time for college, I decided to attend one of my own choosing and selected Tennessee State. I'm glad I did."

Durango took another sip of his coffee. He appreciated her sharing that bit of history with him but felt compelled to ask, "So what does any of that has to do with my asking you to marry me...or why you won't sleep with me once we're married?"

Savannah leaned back in her own chair. "More than anything I want my child to be a part of a large, loving family. I also want my child to know that its father is a part of its life because he wants to be, and not because he was forced to be."

A part of Durango reached out to her, feeling her pain caused by a father who hadn't cared. He was not that kind of man and he was glad she knew it. "I will be a good father to our child, Savannah."

She smiled wryly. "I believe that you will, Durango. Now the issue is whether I believe you will be good to me, as well."

He lifted his brow. "You think I'll mistreat you?"

She shook her head. "No, that's not it. I think you are a man who likes women but I don't want to be just another available body to you, Durango. Not to you or to any man."

Durango placed his teacup down, thinking that if she expected an apology from him for all the women he'd enjoyed before meeting her, she could forget it. Like he'd told her before, what was in the past should stay in the past, unless…

His stomach tightened at the thought that she might assume he would mess around on her. He met her gaze. "Are you worried about me being unfaithful during the time we're married?"

She met his gaze. "That has never crossed my mind. Should it have?"

"No."

He was glad it hadn't crossed her mind because even if she did deny him bedroom rights, he would never give her a reason to question his fidelity. He shook his head. If nothing else, since that night they'd spent together, Savannah had shown him that was definitely a difference between women. Some were only made to bed and some were meant to wed. Savannah, whether she knew it or not, was one of the marrying kind.

She deserved more than a short-term marriage. She deserved a husband who would love and pamper her, for better or for worse and for the rest of her life. A smart man would be good to her and treat her right. Someone who would treat her like a woman of her caliber should be treated. And more importantly, he should be a man who could introduce her to the pleasures men and women shared, pleasures she was denying herself.

He would never forget that night when she had gotten an orgasm. She had acted as if it had been her first one and she hadn't expected the magnitude of the explosion that had ripped through her body. And now he was glad he had shared that with her. But he wanted to share other things with her, as well. And she was wrong if she thought them sleeping together would just be for his benefit. Somehow he had to convince her it would be for her benefit, as well. She needed to understand that a woman has needs just like a man. If nothing else, he needed to prove that to her.

But now was not the time to make waves. He was fairly certain there would be opportunities for what he had in mind before and after their wedding, and he planned to take advantage of both.

"I think of you as more than an available body, Savannah," he said truthfully. "And I'm sorry that you see things that way. In my book, there's nothing wrong with men and women who like and respect each other satisfying their needs, needs they might not be able to control...especially when they're alone together."

He sighed. She was listening to everything he said yet he could tell his discussion of needs was foreign to her. She might have experienced wanting and desire in her lifetime, but she hadn't had to tackle the full-fledged need that sent some women out to shop for certain types of sex toys.

He studied her, watched how her fingertips softly stroked the side of her cup. Her light touch made him wish that she would stroke him the same way. He realized that although she had no idea what the gesture was doing to him, he was excruciatingly aware of her. She looked beautiful just sitting there, absorbing his words yet not fully understanding what he meant.

But eventually she would understand.

"However, if you prefer that we don't share a bed at any time during our marriage, then I will abide by your wishes." Even as he said those words, in his heart he intended that in time her wishes would become the same as his.

She smiled, appearing at ease with what he had said. "So I guess the only other thing we need to agree on is when the marriage will take place and where we'll live afterward."

He nodded. "Like I told you, I'm flexible as far as living arrangements but I think we should get married right away, considering you're already almost two months along."

Savannah did agree with the need to move forward with their marriage but she didn't want him to have to take a leave of absence from his job because of her. It would be easier for her to move to Montana. She could do freelance work anywhere. He could only do his work as a ranger here.

"I think I'd rather live out here, if you don't mind."

That surprised him. A city girl in the mountains? "What about your job? I thought as a freelance photographer you traveled a lot, all over the country."

"Yes, but being pregnant will slow my travels down a bit. Besides, I think I'll be able to work something out with my boss, if my moving out here won't be a problem with you."

Durango shook his head, still bemused but pleased. "No, it won't be and I think you'll be able to adjust to the weather."

"I think so, too."

A feeling of happiness—one he wasn't ready to analyze—coiled through him as he thought of getting married to the mother of his child. "So, when can we marry?"

Savannah shrugged. "I'll let you make all the arrangements. Just tell me when and where you want me to show up."

"And then afterward you'll move in here with me?"

"Yes, and we'll remain married until the baby is at least six months old, which is probably the time I'll be going back to work. Is that time period okay with you?"

"Yes, that's okay. And you still prefer a small wedding?"

"Yes, the smaller the better. Like I said, I don't have a problem eloping to Vegas. A lot of hoopla isn't necessary," she said.

Durango smiled at her. "All right. Considering everything, omitting the hoopla is the least I can do."

Later that day, while Savannah was taking a nap, Durango had a chance to sit down, unwind and think about her decision to marry him.

She understood, as he did, that short-term was short-term. They weren't talking about "until death do us part" or any nonsense like that. They were talking about him being there during the months of her pregnancy, the delivery and the crucial bonding period with his son or daughter.

Hearing about his marriage would be a shocker to

everyone since the family all knew he'd never intended to ever settle down. But the one thing he did know was that his mother would be elated. She had initiated a campaign to marry her sons off. Jared had been the first to go down in defeat and ever since she'd been eyeing him with gleaming hope in her eyes. It didn't bother him that Sarah Westmoreland would enjoy the taste of victory, at least for a short while.

No matter how brief it would be, Durango wanted to make his marriage to Savannah special. He thought of a place they could elope to rather than Vegas. His brother Ian had recently sold his riverboat and was now the proud owner of a casino resort on Lake Tahoe. Durango hadn't had a chance to check things out for himself, but he'd heard from his brothers and cousins that Ian's place was pretty nice. Perhaps Lake Tahoe would be a classier destination for his and Savannah's quickie wedding.

A smile touched the corners of his lips. He planned on sharing an elopement with Savannah that she wouldn't forget.

Now that her decision had been made, Savannah had to tell someone about it. She would tell the one person with whom she shared all her secrets, her sister, Jessica.

She reached for her cell phone off the nightstand and quickly punched in her sister's number in Atlanta. Jessica answered on the second ring.

"Hello."

"Jess, it's me, Savannah."

"Savannah, how did things go in Montana? What did Durango say when you told him? What are you going to do now that he knows?"

Savannah smiled. She'd known Jessica would be full of questions. "I'm still in Montana. I can't fly out due to a severe snowstorm."

"Where are you staying?"

"With Durango. He offered me a place to stay and I accepted."

"That was nice of him."

"Yes, it was. Besides, we had a lot to talk about. And as for your second question, I think I shocked him when I told him I was pregnant. At first he was in denial but then he came to his senses, and…"

"And?"

"And he asked me to marry him."

"Oh, and what was your answer?"

Savannah knew Jessica's point in asking that question. Jessica knew better than anyone how she felt about marrying as the result of an unexpected pregnancy. Her parents had been a prime example that a marriage based on responsibility rather than love didn't work out. "At first I told him no, and—"

"At first?" Jessica cut in abruptly and asked, "Does that mean you eventually told him yes?"

A slight smile touched Savannah's lips. "Yes, I've decided to marry him, but it's going to be to my baby's advantage and it's only going to be on a temporary basis."

"I don't understand. What's going to be on a temporary basis?"

"Our marriage."

There was a pause and then Jessica said, "Let me get this straight. You and Durango have agreed to marry in name only for just a short while?"

Savannah sighed. "Yes, we've agreed to marry and

stay married until our child is at least six months old. That's about the time I'll be ready to return to work full-time."

"And what about you and Durango during this marriage of convenience?"

"What about us?"

"Will the two of you share a bed?"

"No. Our marriage will only be temporary."

"But the two of you will live together? Under the same roof? In the same house? Breathe the same air?"

Savannah frowned, wondering what Jessica was getting at. "Yes. Is there a problem with that?"

"Savannah, the man is a Westmoreland."

Savannah rolled her eyes upward. "And? Am I missing some point here?"

"Think about it, sis. You've slept with him before."

"Yes, and I wasn't fully in my right mind when I did so."

"And you think you won't desire him without being tipsy?"

"Honestly, Jess, of course I'll desire him! Durango is a sexy man. I might not be as sexually active as some women, but I'm not dead, either. A woman would have to be dead or comatose not to notice Durango. I'll admit that I'm attracted to him but that's as far as things are going to go. I can control my urges. I don't have to be intimate with a man, no matter how sexy he is."

"But we're not talking about any man, Savannah, we're talking about a Westmoreland. Trust me, I know the difference. Once you become involved with one, it won't be easy to deny yourself or to walk away later."

"For crying out loud, no matter what you might

think, Jessica, he's just a regular man," Savannah said, intent on making Jessica understand.

"If he was a regular man you wouldn't be in the situation you're in now. Okay, you did overindulge in champagne that night, but you can't convince me that you weren't hot for him already. You asked me about him just moments before the wedding, remember? You *were* interested. I even saw the heat in your eyes. Durango had gotten inside your head before you'd taken your first sip of champagne. That should tell you something."

Savannah expelled a breath. "It does tell me something. It tells me that I'm attracted to him. I've already admitted that. But what you don't realize is that now I'm immune to him."

"And what about falling in love?"

"Falling in love? Lord, Jessica, you know I'm immune to that, as well, doubly so thanks to our poor excuse for a father. Besides, if I even thought about falling in love with Durango, which I won't, all it will take is for me to remember that the only thing connecting us is the baby. The only reason I'm even considering marrying him is to give my child the things I never had, exposure to a warm and loving large family, which I believe the Westmorelands are, and to give Durango a chance to bond with our child. He really wants that and I feel good that he does. Our father didn't care. He was too busy playing two women to give us the time of day."

"At some point you have to let all that go, Savannah," Jessica said softly. "You can't let what Jeff Claiborne did or didn't do dictate your life or your future."

Savannah swallowed a lump in her throat. Some things were easier to get past than others. Her father's mistreatment of his three kids as well as two good women was one of them. "I can't, Jess, and I honestly don't understand how you can. You lost your mother because of him."

"Yes, but I never thought all men were like him, and neither should you."

When Savannah didn't say anything for a long time, Jessica said, "Savannah?"

"Yes," Savannah answered and then sighed.

"Be careful."

"Be careful of what?"

"Of being surprised by the magnitude of a Westmoreland's charm and appeal. When they decide to lay it on thick, watch out. Whether you want to believe it or not, it's easy to fall in love with a Westmoreland man. Trust me, I know. I never intended to fall in love with Chase, remember? He was supposed to be the enemy. And now I can't imagine living my life without him. I love him so much."

"And I'm happy for you, Jess. But you and I are different people. I never believed in happy endings—you did. Just accept my decision and know that for me it's the right one. When I walk away, that will be it. No love lost because there isn't any. Durango doesn't love me and I don't love him, but we're willing to come together and formulate a relationship for our child."

There was a lengthy pause and Savannah wasn't sure she had convinced her sister she had nothing to worry about, but she hoped that she had.

"So, when will the wedding take place?"

"I told Durango that considering the circumstances, I don't want a lot of fuss. So we're eloping to Vegas or someplace and then we'll tell everyone afterward. In a few months, when I begin looking like a blimp, they'll figure out why we married, anyway."

"And you're okay with that?"

"Sure, I'm okay with it. And for the time being, be happy for me, Jess."

"I am happy for you. Have you told Jennifer and Rico yet?"

"No, not yet. I'm not telling either of them until after the marriage takes place. I don't want anyone to try to talk me out of it. You're the only one I've told. I don't know if Durango will tell anyone in his family."

"And when is the trip to Vegas?"

"I don't know, but I'm sure it will be soon. Probably in the next couple of weeks. Durango wants us to get married right away. But he's warned me that once his family hears about our marriage that his mother will probably want to do a huge reception. I'm okay with that."

"And knowing Jennifer, she'll want to do one, as well."

"And I'll be fine with that, too. It will be simpler if they combine their efforts and host one party together. Mom met Mrs. Westmoreland at your wedding and they hit it off so I can see them getting together and planning a nice celebration."

"Yes, I can see them doing that. I'm getting excited just thinking about it."

Savannah smiled. "Get as excited as you want, as long as you remember the marriage won't last. I'll come out of this the same way I'm going into it."

"And what way is that?"

"With realistic expectations."

Seven

As soon as Savannah walked out of the bedroom and saw Durango, their gazes met. The instant attraction that was always there between them began sizzling toward a slow burn.

She would love to photograph him, would definitely appreciate the image she would capture through the lens of her camera and would tuck the developed pictures away to pull out whenever her wild fantasies kicked into gear.

"How was your nap?"

His question snapped her out of her naughty thoughts. Because she'd gone to sleep right after talking with Jessica, she had closed her eyes with Durango on her mind. She had thought about him, dreamed about him, relived the night they had made love....

"Savannah?"

She quickly realized she hadn't answered him. "The

nap was good. How about if I make dinner tonight? While hunting for saltines the other day I came across all the ingredients I'd need to make spaghetti."

He lifted a concerned eyebrow. "Will that agree with your stomach?"

She chuckled as she dropped down on the sofa, trying to ignore just how sexy he looked with his shoulder leaning against a doorway that separated the living room from the dining area. He was standing with his thumbs hooked in the front pocket of his jeans, and the chambray shirt he was wearing was straining across his muscular chest.

"In the afternoon everything agrees with my stomach, Durango. It's the mornings that I have to worry about. So how does spaghetti sound?" she asked, hoping her voice didn't contain the sizzle that she felt.

He lifted one shoulder in a shrug. "Great, if you're up to it. That will give me a chance to take a shower. And I need to talk to you about a few things."

Savannah's dark brow lifted, which helped to downplay the fluttering she felt in her stomach. "Talk to me about what?"

"While you were resting I took the liberty to make a few calls and check on some things. You did say you were leaving all the arrangements to me and would be fine with everything as long as I left out the hoopla."

"Yes, I did."

"Well, I've made wedding plans and want to discuss them with you, to make sure they meet your approval."

She blinked in surprise. While she'd been napping, he'd evidently been busy. "Wedding plans? Then we definitely need to talk after your shower."

"All right, I'll be back in a minute." Before turning

to leave, he asked, "Are you sure you don't need my help with dinner?"

"No, I can handle things."

"Yes, I'm sure you can," he countered, smiling.

And when he walked out the room she had a feeling that he'd been hinting at more than just her spaghetti.

"Everything tastes good, Savannah."

"Thank you." She tried looking at anything and everything other than the man sitting across the table from her. Doing so was simply too tempting. After glancing out the window and seeing it was still snowing, she scanned the room and took in the beauty of his kitchen and again mentally admired the setup of everything, including the pots that…

"Are you okay?"

His question forced her to do something she hadn't wanted to do. Look directly at him. The moment she did so she felt fiery tingles move down her spine. "Yes, I'm okay. Why do you ask?"

"No particular reason."

Sitting this close to him she could actually smell his scent, one that was all man. But that didn't compare to how he'd looked when he had entered the kitchen after his shower wearing jeans that hung low on his hips and a shirt he hadn't bothered to button.

"Are you ready to talk about the plans I've made?"

His question pulled her mind back from lurking into a territory where it had no business going. "Sure."

He stood and began gathering the dishes off the table. "Instead of going to Vegas I thought it would be nice if we went to Lake Tahoe instead."

She raised an eyebrow. "Lake Tahoe?"

"Yes, my brother Ian recently bought a casino resort there. I heard it's truly spectacular and I would like to take you there."

"Lake Tahoe," she said again, savoring the idea. She had visited the area a few years ago and had thought it was beautiful. She smiled across the table at Durango. "All right. That sounds like a winner to me, so when do you want to do it?"

"Day after tomorrow."

"What!"

He chuckled at her startled expression. "I think Friday would be a perfect day for us to leave for Lake Tahoe. Starting today the weather will begin improving and tomorrow you can—"

"Hold up. Time out. Cut." She caught her breath for a moment and then said, "Durango, there's no way I can marry you on Friday. I have to go back home and take care of a few things. I have to plan for the wedding. I have to—"

"We're eloping, remember? And besides, I thought you didn't want a lot of hoopla."

He had her there. "I don't, but I hadn't thought about getting married *this* soon."

"The sooner the better, don't you think? You're a couple of months already. Jayla began really sticking out there by the fourth month. I remember when I went home for my father's birthday during Easter and she was huge, almost as big as a house."

Savannah raised her eyes to the ceiling, hoping he had the good sense not to mention such a thing to Jayla. Even pregnant, women were sensitive when it came to their weight. "She was carrying twins, Durango, for heaven's sake."

"And how do you know you aren't? Multiple births run in my family. My father is the twin to Chase's father and both of them had twins. Then Uncle Corey had triplets, so anything is possible."

That wasn't what Savannah wanted to hear. She much preferred having one healthy baby, but of course she would gladly accept whatever she got. "I couldn't possibly get ready for Lake Tahoe by Friday. I didn't bring any clothes here with me and I would need to purchase some things."

"There're several stores in Bozeman that will have everything you need. Tomorrow can be a shopping day."

Savannah felt rushed and decided to let him know it. "I feel like you're rushing me," she said briskly.

A smile touched his lips. "In a way I am. Now that we've decided to do it, why wait? I want us to marry as soon as possible."

She couldn't help wondering why. Did he think she would change her mind or something? She was carrying his baby, and until she'd shown up and announced that fact, he hadn't been interested in marriage. She had thought she would have at least a couple of weeks, maybe even a month before they actually did anything. She'd assumed she would leave tomorrow to return to Philadelphia and they would make plans for the wedding over the phone. This was definitely not what she had expected.

"Savannah, why are you hesitating? We should move forward and get things over with."

Get things over with? Well, he certainly didn't have to make it sound like marrying her was something being forced upon him. No one had asked him to do it. Getting married was his idea and not hers. She was about to tell him just that when he did something she hadn't expected. He tugged her hand and pulled her out of her chair, wrapping his arms around her and pulling her against him.

Startled, her head came up the moment her body pressed against his. Very little space separated them. A smile touched the corners of his mouth for a few seconds before he said softly, "You're trying to be difficult, aren't you?"

She swallowed. It wasn't easy to gaze into the dark eyes holding hers captive. "Not intentionally."

"Then why the cold feet? I've already checked the airlines and there are plenty of flights available, and I've talked to my brother Ian."

At her frown he said, "And yes, I told him we decided to get married, but I didn't tell him why. He said that he would love to have us as his guests for the weekend. He's making all the necessary arrangements."

He studied her features for a moment then asked, "Are you having second thoughts about eloping, Savannah? Do you prefer having a small wedding here so that we could invite our families?"

"No," she said quickly. "I still prefer keeping things simple. I guess I'm hesitating because it never dawned on me that I might be returning to Philadelphia a married woman."

"Then I guess you aren't prepared to return to Philadelphia with a husband in tow, either."

His words were a shocker. "You're going back with me?"

"Yes. You'll have to introduce me to your family sometime."

Her head was reeling from the thought of him returning to Philadelphia with her. "You've already met my family at Chase and Jessica's wedding."

"Yes, but I met them as Chase's cousin, not as your husband. Besides, we'll be newlyweds and it will seem strange for us not to be together."

"Yes, but—"

"And I want to take you home to Atlanta, as well, to meet my family. Not as Jessica's sister but as my wife. Although everyone will probably reach their own conclusions as to why we eloped and got married, it's really none of their business. We'll tell them that we met at the wedding, fell madly in love and decided to get married."

Savannah couldn't help but smile at Durango's ridiculous statement. There was no way anyone would believe such a thing, and from the mischievous grin touching his lips, he knew that, as well.

"Let's keep them guessing," Durango said, chuckling. "Our decision doesn't concern anyone but us."

Savannah couldn't help but agree with that, especially after her conversation with Jessica. Everything he was saying made sense. Now that they had decided to marry, why prolong things? "Fine, if you think we can pull it off, then Friday is fine."

"Good. And there's something else you'll need to do tomorrow."

"What?"

"Visit the doctor in town. I've already made you an appointment for tomorrow morning."

Savannah pulled back slightly and frowned. "Why?

Don't you believe I'm pregnant? Or do you want to have it verified before going through with the marriage ceremony?"

"No, that's not it," he said tightly. "I just want the doctor to check you out to make sure you're okay. You gave me a scare this morning and I just want to make sure you and the baby are fine."

Savannah met his gaze and saw the sincerity in his eyes and knew he had spoken the truth. "Okay," she finally said. "I'll go to the doctor for a checkup if it will make you happy."

"It will," he said. "And thank you."

Savannah drew in a deep breath. She needed space from Durango and took a step back. "I'll get started on the dishes and—"

"No, you did the cooking so it's only fair that I clean up the kitchen."

"Durango, I can manage to—"

"Savannah, that's the way it's going to be. Just relax. You'll have more than enough to do over the next couple of days, and it seems the weather is going to cooperate."

She glanced out the window and saw it had stopped snowing. This was the break in the weather she'd been waiting for. But now, instead of packing to return home to Philly, she'd be preparing for a wedding.

"If you're sure that you can handle the dishes by yourself, then I need to call and talk with my boss. I had told him I would be back in the office on Monday."

"Okay." When she turned to leave he said, "And Savannah?"

She turned back around. "Yes?"

"I planned for us to stay in the same suite but it has two bedrooms. Will that be a problem?"

She swallowed deeply as her gaze held his. "No, that won't be a problem as long as there will be two bedrooms."

The smile that suddenly touched his lips made her stomach flutter and made heat flow all over her. "Then we're all set. I'll call the airlines and book us a flight."

They were eloping to Lake Tahoe.

Durango's announcement of last night was the main reason for Savannah's sleepless night. And the magnitude of it must have shocked her system because she had awakened the next morning without any feelings of nausea.

However, it seemed that Durango intended to be prepared because when she opened her eyes, she found him sitting in the chair beside her bed with a plate of saltines and a cup of tea all ready for her.

"Good morning."

The sensuous sound of his voice so early in the morning sent shivers all through her, and the concerned smile that touched his lips wasn't helping matters, either.

"Good morning," she said, pulling herself up in bed. Although she appreciated his kindness and thoughtfulness, she would have much preferred if he had given her a minute or two to freshen up. She would have liked to comb her hair and wash the sleep from her eyes.

"Are you feeling okay this morning?"

"Yes, thanks for asking. For some reason I'm not feeling nauseated." She decided not to tell him her suspicions on the reason why.

"I'm glad to hear that." He then nodded his head toward the fireplace. "I tried keeping it warm in here during the night."

Her gaze followed his to the roaring flame. "Thank you." Because she hadn't been able to sleep, she had been aware of each and every time he had come into her room and checked the heat.

"This is going to be a busy day for us since we'll be flying out first thing in the morning."

Savannah's gaze returned to his. "I imagine that it will be."

"After our doctor visit, I'll take you to the mall. I figured you would probably want to shop alone, so I'll use that time to pay McKinnon a visit and then come back later for you. You do remember my best friend McKinnon, don't you?"

"Yes, I remember him." She definitely remembered McKinnon Quinn, just like she was sure a number of other women would. With his beautiful golden-brown complexion and thick ponytail, she had admired his handsome features that reflected his mixed-race ancestry. She had actually blinked twice when she'd first seen him because the man had been simply gorgeous. But even with McKinnon's striking good looks, it had been Durango who had caught her eye and held it.

"I guess I'll leave you alone so you can get dressed now," Durango said, standing and placing the tea and saltines on the nightstand.

It took fierce concentration to keep Savannah's mind on their conversation and not on Durango as he got out of the chair. He was dressed in a pair of jeans, a pullover sweater and a pair of black leather boots. She didn't care how many times she saw him dressed that way, but each time his appearance grabbed her attention. "Thanks for the crackers and tea," she said.

Durango smiled. "Don't mention it."

Savannah's breath caught in her throat from that one smile, and when he turned his head to glance out the window, she grabbed that opportunity to study him some more. His eyes were focused on the mountains as if weighing a problem of some kind, and she wondered if perhaps he thought the good weather wouldn't last. When he turned his head he caught her staring at him and for a brief breath of a moment she felt the sizzle that always seemed to hang in the air between them.

"I'd better be going. There's a couple of things I need to check on outside before we leave," he said and, as if tearing his gaze from hers, he glanced over at the fireplace. "That thing keeps this room pretty hot, doesn't it?"

She followed his gaze. It was on the tip of her tongue to say that at the moment she thought it was him, and not the fireplace, that made the room pretty hot. Instead she said, "Yes, it does."

Savannah had to admit, however, that she did enjoy sleeping in a room with a fireplace. She had gotten used to the stark smell of burning wood, the sound of loose pieces crackling as they caught fire, and more than anything, she liked the comforting warmth the fire provided.

"Do you think you'll be able to eat any food this morning?" Durango asked, interrupting her thoughts.

She frowned, deciding not to chance it. "I'd better not try it. Those saltines and tea will do just fine. Thanks."

Moments after Durango had left the room, Savannah

sat on the edge of her bed thinking about all the things she had to do to get ready for tomorrow. Just thinking about everything made her feel exhausted. But she was determined to get through the day and in a way, she was looking forward to her visit to the doctor.

A quiver raced through her stomach at the thought that Durango would be there, too, sharing the experience with her.

Eight

"So how's the baby?" Durango asked the doctor nervously.

Lying flat on her back on the examination table, Savannah shifted her gaze to Durango, who was standing beside her. She heard the deep concern in his voice and saw how his eyebrows came together in a tense expression.

She then switched her gaze to Dr. Patrina Foreman. Dr. Foreman was a lot younger than Savannah had expected. She was a very attractive woman and she appeared to be about twenty-eight. Within minutes of talking to her, Savannah was convinced that even though she might be young, she was definitely competent. Dr. Foreman had explained that her mother, grandmother and great-grandmother had been midwives, but that she had decided to complete medical school to offer her patients the best of both worlds. She could provide modern medical treatments as well as the type of care and personal attention that midwives were known to give.

Dr. Foreman lifted her gaze from applying the gel on Savannah's stomach and smiled before saying, "Listen to this for a moment and then tell me what you think."

And then they heard it, the soft thumping sound of their child's heartbeat, for the first time. Hearing the steady little drumbeat did something to Savannah, touched her in a way she hadn't expected and made her realize that she really and truly was going to have a baby.

Tears, something else she hadn't expected, came into her eyes and she glanced up at Durango and knew he was just as moved by the sound as she was. He reached out and firmly touched her shoulder, and at that moment she knew that no matter how they did or didn't feel about each other, her pregnancy was real and they were listening to valid proof of just how real it was. There was no doubt that hearing the sound was a life-altering experience for both of them.

"You hadn't heard it before?" Durango asked softly.

"No. This is my first time."

"There's nothing like parents hearing the fetal heartbeat for the first time," Dr. Foreman said quietly. "There's always something special and exciting about it. The baby's heartbeat is strong and sounds healthy to me."

Durango chuckled. "Yes, it does, doesn't it? This is all rather new to me and I was kind of worried."

"And you have every right to be concerned, but it seems mother and baby are doing just fine," Dr. Foreman replied, removing the instrument from Savannah's stomach. "Make sure that you continue to take your prenatal vitamins, Savannah."

"And what about all that vomiting she's been doing?" Durango asked, wanting to know.

Dr. Foreman glanced at him. "Morning sickness is caused by the sudden increase of hormones during pregnancy and is very common early in the pregnancy, but it's usually gone by the fourth month." She smiled at Savannah and said, "So, hopefully you won't have to suffer too much longer."

"I prefer she didn't suffer at all. And what about the baby? Will it be hurt by it?" Durango asked, in a tone that said he really needed Dr. Foreman's assurance.

"It shouldn't, but of course it can become a problem if Savannah can't keep any foods or fluids down or if she begins to lose weight. Otherwise, morning sickness is a positive sign that the pregnancy is progressing."

Dr. Foreman then opened a drawer and pulled out a package and handed it to Savannah. "This might help. It's the same type of acupressure wristbands that doctors give out on cruise ships to prevent seasickness. A lot of my patients swear that wearing it helps to reduce the morning sickness."

For the next ten to fifteen minutes, Dr. Foreman answered all of Savannah and Durango's questions. Then she congratulated them when Durango mentioned they were getting married.

"I really like her," Savannah told Durango when they left the doctor's office. "And I hadn't expected her to be so young."

Durango smiled as he ushered Savannah out the building to where he had parked his truck. "Yes, Trina is young but I've heard that she is one of the best. She was born and raised around these parts and her husband Perry was the sheriff. He was killed a few years ago in the line of duty while trying to arrest an escaped convict."

"Oh, how awful."

Durango nodded. "Yes, it was. Perry was a good person and everyone liked and respected him. He and Trina had been childhood sweethearts."

Durango opened the door to his truck and assisted Savannah in settling in and buckling her seat belt. "Was it a coincidence or did you deliberately buy this particular SUV?" she asked grinning. It was ironic that his name was Durango and that was also the model of the vehicle that he drove.

He chuckled as he snapped her seat belt in place. "Not a coincidence. I thought I'd milk it for all it's worth since Dodge decided to name a vehicle after me," he said arrogantly, giving her that smile that made her stomach spin. "Besides, we're both known to give smooth and unforgettable rides," he added softly while gazing into her eyes.

For a moment Savannah couldn't speak since she of all people knew about the smoothness, as well as the intensity, of Durango's ride. The very thought was generating earth-shattering memories of the time he had pleasured her in bed.

She watched as he walked around the front of the truck to get into the driver's seat. "You're taking me to the mall now?" she asked, trying to get her heartbeat back on track. If she was having trouble keeping her thoughts off him now, she didn't want to think how things would be once they were married.

"Yes, I'm taking you to the Gallatin Valley Mall," Durango said, pulling out of the parking lot and returning her attention. "You should be able to find everything you need there. Do you want me to stay and shop with you?"

"No, I'll be fine," she quickly said, knowing she needed her space for a while. "If there's one thing a woman knows how to do on her own it's shop."

Stealing a glance at him she couldn't help wondering how he really felt about marrying her and suddenly needed to know that he was still okay with their plans.

"Durango?"

"Yes?"

The truck had come to a stop at a traffic light and she knew his gaze was on her but she refused to look at him. Instead she looked straight ahead. "Are you sure getting married is what you really want to do?" she asked as calmly as she could.

"Yes, I'm sure," he said in a voice so low and husky, Savannah couldn't help but turn to meet his gaze. Then in a way she wished she hadn't when she saw the deep, dark intensity in his eyes. He then smiled and that smile touched her, and she couldn't help but return it.

"If I wasn't before, Savannah, I am now, especially after listening to our baby's heartbeat. God, that was an awesome experience. And according to Trina, it has all the vital organs it will need already. It's not just a cluster of cells but a real human being. A being that we created and I want to connect to it more so than ever."

Savannah sighed in relief. The last thing she wanted was for him to ever regret marrying her. She was satisfied that he wouldn't.

* * *

Bozeman, one of the most diverse small towns in the Rocky Mountains, was known for its hospitality and was proud of its numerous ski resorts. It was a city that attracted not only tourists, but also families wanting to plant their roots in a place that offered good quality of life.

Durango drove straight to the mall and parked the truck. He even took the time to walk Savannah inside, saying there were a couple of things he needed to purchase for himself. He gave her his cell phone number in case she finished shopping early so she could reach him.

Once they parted ways, Savannah became a woman on a mission as she went from store to store. Within a few hours she had purchased everything she needed and had indulged herself by getting a few things she really hadn't needed, like a few sexy nightgowns she had purchased from Victoria's Secret. It wasn't as if Durango would ever see her in any of them, but still, she couldn't help herself. She liked buying sexy things.

A few hours later Savannah had made all of her purchases, and contacted Durango on his cell phone. He told her he had just pulled into the parking lot and would meet her at the food court in the center of the mall. He suggested that they grab dinner at a really good restaurant there.

She had been in the food court for only a few minutes when she glanced across the way and saw him. Her pulse quickened. There was no way she could discount the fact that he was a devastatingly handsome man, and she wasn't the only female who noticed. As he crossed the mall in long, confident strides, several heads turned to watch him, and for a moment Savannah felt both pride and a tinge of jealousy.

She quickly dismissed the latter emotion. He wasn't hers and she wasn't his. But still, as he continued to walk toward her, closing the distance separating them, she saw the look in his eyes, deciphered the way he was looking at her with that steady dark gaze of his. It was the same way he had looked at her the night of Chase and Jessica's wedding.

And as if it was the most natural thing to do, when he reached her he leaned down and kissed her. Surprised, she returned the brief, but thorough kiss while her heart thumped ominously in her chest.

"Did you get a lot accomplished today?" he asked softly against her moist lips.

Not able to speak at first, she nodded. Then she said breathlessly, "Yes, I think I have everything I'm going to need. And I think I found an appropriate dress for tomorrow."

Durango chuckled as he took her hand in his and led her toward the restaurant where they would dine. "I'm sure it's more than appropriate. I bet it's perfect and I can't wait to see you in it."

Later that night while packing, Savannah had to admit that it had been a simply wonderful day. First the visit to the doctor and then her shopping trip to the mall and last, having dinner with Durango at that restaurant. The food had been delicious and Durango's company had been excellent. Over a candlelight dinner he had told her about his partnership with McKinnon's horse farm and how well it was doing.

Closing her luggage, Savannah smiled when she recalled the message Jessica had left on Durango's answering machine, telling them to expect her and Chase at Lake Tahoe tomorrow. A part of Savannah had been both elated and relieved that elopement or not, a stubborn Jessica would not let her get married without her sister being there. Durango also seemed pleased that his cousin was coming, as well.

She looked up when she heard the knock on her bedroom door. "Come in."

Durango entered, dressed in a pair of jogging pants and a T-shirt with a towel wrapped around his neck. "I was about to get into the hot tub and was wondering if you would like to join me."

"But it's cold outside."

He smiled ruefully. "Yes, but once you get into the tub you'll forget how cold it is. It's the best thing to stimulate sore, aching muscles. Try it. I guarantee that you'll like it."

Savannah thought of all the walking she had done earlier that day at the mall and decided a soak in the hot tub sounded good. But still…

"Is it large enough for the both of us to fit comfortably?" The thought of being crammed into a hot tub with Durango was too much to think about.

"Yes, it can hold five to six people without any problems."

She nodded. Good. He could stay on his side of the tub and she could stay on hers. "All right, then let me change into a swimming suit." She had bought one that day at the mall and had to dig it out from the suitcase.

After Durango left Savannah changed her clothes, thankful that the swimming suit she had purchased was a one-piece and wasn't overly provocative. The attraction between her and Durango was bad enough without adding fuel to an already hot fire.

"For a moment I thought I was going to have to come back inside to get you."

She chuckled and quickly padded on bare feet across the deck to the hot tub. "Sorry. My mom called right when I was about to come outside."

His eyebrows lifted. "Did you tell her about our plans for tomorrow?"

"Yes," Savannah said as she quickly dispensed with her robe and eased inside the tub, deliberately sinking as far down as she could and letting a sound of "ahh" ease from between her lips. Once she got settled in a comfortable position she added, "I didn't give her a lot of details and told her we can have a long discussion when she returns from Paris. But she is very astute in reading between the lines, so I'm sure she has an idea why we're having a quick wedding."

Durango studied her eyes since her face was the only part of her he could see. She had water covering her entire body, from her shoulders to her toes. She was almost completely submerged.

"Did your mom know we'd been involved?" he asked, wishing he had X-ray vision that would enable him to see her body through the water. But he had caught a glimpse of her curves when she had removed her robe. Although she had tried to be quick about it and to not draw any attention to herself, she had failed miserably. Her swimsuit was sexy, and the cut was a snug fit that showed off her shapely thighs and bottom.

"If she does it's not because I've told her anything,"

Savannah said, cutting into his thoughts. "However, she did mention when we met for lunch last month that she couldn't help noticing that we were having a hard time keeping our eyes off each other at the wedding." She decided not to add that her mother had also noticed when the two of them had left the reception together.

"Hey, this feels nice," she said, liking how the hot water seemed to penetrate the tired muscles of her body. "And you were right. I don't feel how cold the temperature is."

"I'm glad. And by the way, you can come from hiding under the water. I promise not to jump your bones if you do," he said slowly, grinning.

She met his gaze and smiled sheepishly. "I didn't think that you would. I was merely making sure I wouldn't freeze to death."

"And now that you know that you won't?"

She took a deep breath and eased more of her body out of the water. When the hot, bubbling, swirling water came to her waist like it did his, she felt a sizzling sensation flow down her spine and settle in the pit of her stomach. He was staring at her. Her bathing suit was decent, but it was fashioned in a style that made anyone aware of the fullness of her breasts.

"I like your swimming suit. At least what I've seen of it so far," he said. His voice was low, intimate.

"Thanks." She then glanced around. "So what made you decide to put this hot tub in?"

He gave her an intent look, knowing she was trying to change the subject. "It was an easy decision since I was taking advantage of one of the natural hot springs located on my property."

"Oh, you have others?"

He grinned, knowing he had told her that already. "Yes, but don't expect me to show them to you tonight," he said, leaning back against the wall of the tub and deliberately stretching out one of his legs. He made it seem like an accident, an innocent mistake when his thigh touched her thigh. She gasped and slowly eased back to give him more space.

"Going someplace?" he asked with a totally innocent look on his face.

"No, I'm just trying to give you more room."

"I don't need more room."

"Could have fooled me," she muttered under her breath.

"You say something?"

She glanced over at him. "No, just thinking out loud."

Before she could blink he had pushed away from the wall and had glided over to her, putting his face inches from hers. "Now what did you say, Savannah?"

Savannah pulled in a sharp intake of breath. Not only was Durango's face near hers, but she could feel the heat from his entire body. He was within touching distance. He was making the already hot water that much hotter.

"Did I ever tell you how much I like kissing you, Savannah?" he asked.

A shudder of desire ran through her, first starting at her toes and easing its way to the top of her head. "I don't recall if you have or not," she said silkily, watching his lips inch even closer.

"Well, let me go on record and say that I do. You have a unique taste," he said in a deep, husky tone.

"I do?"

"Yes. It's so tantalizingly sweet that I can feast on it for hours."

Another shudder ran through her. "No man has ever told me that before."

He smiled. "Then maybe you haven't kissed the right man."

"Maybe."

"And although you haven't given me any bedroom rights while we're married, you haven't denied me kissing rights, have you?" he asked in a sensual tone.

"Ahh, no." *But maybe I should,* she quickly thought.

"Good, because I'm going to enjoy kissing you whenever I can."

She held her breath when he leaned forward, wrapped his arms around her waist and took the tip of his tongue and began slowly, sensuously, passionately tracing the outline of her mouth.

She moaned deep and eased his name from between her lips just moments before he slipped his tongue inside her mouth. Moaning more, she returned his kiss as their tongues met, mingled and stroked. The signals they were exchanging were intimately familiar, and all it took was the shift of their legs to bring their bodies right smack together, making her feel the very essence of his heat. She knew exactly what that huge, hot engorged body part pressed against her midsection meant.

Savannah wanted to pull back, stop playing with fire, cease indulging in temptation, but she couldn't. Her legs felt weak, her thighs were becoming a quivering mass and her mouth was definitely getting branded the Durango way. And when he reached up and touched the tip of her breasts through the soft and clingy material of her swimsuit, she almost lost her bearing. She would have done so if his hands weren't still around her waist, holding her close.

He pulled back slightly and whispered hotly against her moist lips, "I also like touching you. You feel hot all over."

It was on the tip of her tongue to say that thanks to him she *was* hot all over, but at that moment he leaned forward and took that same tongue into his mouth again, ending further conversation. Her heartbeat kicked up a notch when his hand moved from her waist and slid lower and when he shifted their bodies so he could sufficiently caress the area between her legs, through the soft material of her swimsuit, she almost cried out at the sensations he elicited.

"I know this part of you is off-limits," he said in a deep, throaty voice that sent even more heat running through her. "But I can tell it wants me. It wants how I can make it feel, Savannah. It's hot for me, the same way I'm hot for you. For two months I've lain in my bed at night and thought about us, how we were that night, how good we were together and how good we could be again."

While he was talking, drumming up memories, his thumb continued to caress her, driving her mad, insane with desire and her head fell forward to his chest, her breathing became choppy and her mind was overtaken by passion.

"It's going to be hard for us to share space being such passionate individuals and not want to do something about it, don't you think?" he asked hotly against her ear.

"Yes, I'm sure it will be," she agreed, easing the words from between her lips.

"But I'm honor bound to abide by your wishes and I will…unless you change your mind and give me the word to do otherwise. And then there won't be any stopping me, Savannah."

Savannah didn't know what to say. And when she thought of what would happen if she ever changed her mind as well as the movement of his fingers on her, a needy ache flamed to life between her legs. And when a shudder began passing through her again, igniting every cell in her body, sending sensations rushing through her, she called out his name. Just with the use of his fingers he had pushed her over the edge, giving her the big "O" without fully penetrating the barriers of her clothing.

Durango gently pulled on her hair to bring her face back to his and he kissed her, literally drank his name from her lips, as his hungry and demanding mouth devoured her, giving her a taste of what she would be missing, and giving him a thorough taste of her.

Savannah forced her mouth away from his when breathing became a necessity. The first thing she noticed was that sometime during their kiss she had wrapped her legs around him. She didn't remember doing it but Durango *had* been kissing her senseless and the only thing she did remember was the magnitude of that kiss, the explosiveness of it.

She inhaled deeply. Jessica was right. This wasn't a regular man. This was a Westmoreland and they didn't do anything halfway. She had a pregnancy to prove it. What other man could make a woman scream his name in ecstasy while still wearing clothes?

She looked up at him to say something and he leaned forward and kissed her again. This kiss was slow, lingering and just as hot as the kisses that he'd lavished on her before.

When he pulled back his dark eyes held her with deep intensity. And his voice was strained when he said, "I meant what I said, Savannah. I want to make love to you again, but unless you give me the word, kissing is as far as it will go between us."

She nodded and closed her eyes, knowing he would respect the boundaries she had set. But she also knew that he intended to use his kisses to break down her defenses. When she felt him easing away, she opened her eyes and watched him get out of the hot tub. His wet swimming trunks clung to his body like a second layer of skin, and the evidence of his desire for her was still evident.

He was silent while he toweled off, watching her watch him. He smiled knowingly. "Tomorrow is our wedding day and regardless of the reason that brought us to this point, Savannah, I intend to make it a special day for you. For the both of us."

Moments later when the patio door closed behind him, Savannah sank deeper into the water, already feeling the loss of Durango's heat. Whether she wanted to or not, a part of her couldn't help but look forward to tomorrow, the day when—even though it would be temporary—she would become Mrs. Durango Westmoreland.

Nine

The following day when they pulled up to the entrance of the Rolling Cascade Casino and Resort, Savannah was at a loss for words. As a photographer she had traveled to many picturesque sites, but she thought nothing could have prepared her for the car ride from Reno to Ian Westmoreland's exclusive resort on Lake Tahoe.

She and Durango had flown into Reno and had rented a car for the drive to Lake Tahoe. They decided to take what he declared to be the scenic route; the panoramic view was spectacular and more than once she had asked Durango to stop the car so she could take pictures of the snowcapped mountains, the enormous boulders and the clusters of shrubs and pine trees that grew almost down to the lake.

Just minutes from Stateline, Nevada, the Rolling Cascade looked different from the other sprawling casinos they had passed. Ian's resort was a beautifully designed building that overlooked Lake Tahoe and was surrounded by a number of specialty shops, clothing stores and a myriad of restaurants.

Durango had explained that the Cascade had been vacant for almost a year after it was discovered that the previous owner had been using the casino as a front for an illegal operation. When it had gone up for sale, Ian and his investors had been ready to bring their casino business on land. Hurricane Katrina had made it impossible to continue his riverboat's route along the Mississippi from New Orleans to Memphis.

Ian had remodeled the establishment to be a small community within itself. Having been open for six months, the resort had already shown amazing profits and was giving plenty of stiff competition to the likes of the Las Vegas–style casinos situated close by.

"This place is simply beautiful," Savannah said when Durango brought the car to a stop. Within seconds, members of the resort's staff were there to greet them and to assist with their bags.

Durango smiled as he placed a muscled arm around her shoulders as they walked inside the building. The Cascade's inside was just as impressive as its outside. Durango stopped and glanced around, letting out a low whistle. Moments later he said, "Ian really did it up this time. I think he's found his calling."

"I think so, too, brother."

Both Durango and Savannah turned to find a smiling Ian standing directly behind them. He gave Durango an affectionate bear hug and leaned over and brushed a kiss on Savannah's cheek. "I'm glad you like what you see," Ian said and smiled.

"We do," Savannah replied, returning his smile and thinking that all the Westmoreland brothers and cousins resembled each other. They were all tall, dark and handsome; however, Ian's neatly trimmed short beard added a rakish look to his features. "And I appreciate you having us here," she added.

Ian grinned. "No reason to thank me. It's about time Durango came down from the mountains and went someplace other than Atlanta. Besides, it's not every day that a Westmoreland gets married. Come on and let me get the both of you checked in. I have the wedding chapel reserved for five o'clock. That will give you time to rest and relax a bit before the ceremony."

"Have Chase and Jessica arrived yet?" Durango asked as he and Savannah followed Ian over to the check-in counter.

"Yes, they got in a few hours ago and last time I checked they were getting ready to take a stroll around the shops."

A huge smile then touched Ian's lips. "And I have a surprise for you, Durango."

"What?"

"I got a call from McKinnon. That appointment he had scheduled for today got canceled and he was able to get a flight out and will be arriving just in time for the wedding."

Durango smiled, pleased his best friend would make the wedding after all.

Less than ten minutes later Durango and Savannah were stepping inside what Ian had told them was a vacant owner's suite, which to Savannah's way of thinking looked more like an exclusive condo with its three bedrooms, two full baths, gigantic fireplace, kitchen area and beautiful balcony that overlooked Lake Tahoe.

Savannah gave an inward sigh of relief at seeing the three bedrooms, although one of them she assumed due to its size was intended to be a master suite. She didn't want a repeat of the temptation she had faced the previous night while in the hot tub with Durango, and was grateful for the spaciousness of the place.

"I'll let you choose whichever bedroom you prefer," Durango said, closing the door behind him.

She turned around and smiled sheepishly. "Because of all the stuff I brought along with me, I'll take the biggest of the three bedrooms, if you don't mind."

He chuckled. "No, I don't mind." He glanced at his watch. "We have a few hours to kill. Do you want to take a walk around the lake?"

"I'd love to, and it was nice of Ian to let us use this suite, wasn't it?"

Durango grinned. "Yes, he can be a nice enough guy when he wants to be. But there are times when he's known to be a pain in the ass."

Savannah knew he was kidding. Anyone who hung around the Westmorelands for any length of time could tell they were a close-knit group. "Give me a few minutes to freshen up, okay?"

"Sure."

When she reached her bedroom, Durango called out to her.

"Ian mentioned there's a private hot tub on the twelfth floor if we wanted to try it out," he said.

Images of the two of them in the hot tub last night and the heated kiss they had shared floated into Savannah's mind. Just the thoughts made a tingly feeling settle in the pit of her stomach. "I think I'll pass on that."

"You sure?" he asked, grinning, making her remember in blatant details their hot-tub antics of the night before.

"I'm positive."

"If I didn't know the score I'd think you and Durango were excited about getting married."

Savannah glanced at her sister as she slipped into her wedding dress. She and Durango had run into Chase and Jessica while touring the grounds around the lake. Jessica had suggested that Savannah get dressed for the ceremony in the suite she and Durango shared. Durango would dress in Chase and Jessica's room. That way the bride and groom wouldn't see each other in their wedding attire before they were married.

"You're imagining things. Durango and I came to an agreement to do what's in the best interest of our child. That's the only reason we're getting married."

Jessica Claiborne Westmoreland laughed, reached out and hugged her sister and said, "Hey, whatever, I still think the two of you look good together."

Savannah looked at Jessica in mild exasperation. "And I told you not to get any ideas, Jess."

"If you don't want me to get any ideas, then how about explaining these?" she said, gesturing to all the sexy sleepwear Savannah had unpacked earlier. "If these aren't for Durango's enjoyment then who are they for?" she asked, picking up one of the negligees.

"For me. You know how much I like wearing sexy things to bed," Savannah said, reaching out and taking the item from Jessica and tossing it back on the bed. "Since Durango and I won't be sharing a bed, what I sleep in is no business of his."

Jessica tipped her head, regarded Savannah thoughtfully and said, "You still haven't gotten it yet, have you?"

"Gotten what?"

"The fact that a Westmoreland man isn't anyone to play with. How long do you think the two of you will be able to fight this intense attraction? Even today he was looking at you when he thought you weren't looking and you were looking at him when you thought he wasn't looking. The two of you were doing the same thing at my wedding."

"And your point?"

"The point is that you know what happened as soon as the two of you were alone and behind closed doors."

"We indulged in too much champagne that night, Jess. That won't happen this time because I don't plan to consume any alcohol while I'm pregnant."

"There's another way a woman can get tipsy, Savannah. There is such a thing as being overtaken by sexual chemistry and losing your head," she said, letting her gaze stray to the nightgowns once again.

"I don't plan to lose my head."

"What about your heart?"

"That, either. Now tell me how I look."

Jessica glanced up and fell silent. She had seen the short, white lace dress on the hanger and thought it looked okay, but on Savannah the dress looked like it had been made just for her, and just for this special occasion. Savannah looked so beautiful it almost brought tears to Jessica's eyes.

"Well, what do you think?" Savannah asked when Jessica didn't say anything.

"I think that you look simply beautiful and I'm sorry that Jennifer isn't here to see you," Jessica said, almost choking with emotion.

"Hey, knock it off, Jess. This wedding is no big deal. The only reason we're getting married is because I'm pregnant…remember?"

Jessica reached out to pick up another skimpy piece of lingerie only to have Savannah shoo her hand away. She chuckled and then asked, "So when are you going to let Rico know you're a married woman?"

Savannah closed her luggage with a firm click. "Durango and I will be calling and telling everybody the news when we get back. We had hoped to take off for Philly and Atlanta next week to drop the bomb in person, but because one of the park rangers is out on medical leave, it will be another month before Durango can take time off work. Maybe that's just as well since it will give everyone a chance to get used to the idea."

"I can't wait to see the Westmorelands' reaction when they hear the news. Durango is the last person anyone would have thought would marry."

"Yes, but let me remind you again that the only reason he's doing so now is because I'm pregnant, and don't you forget it."

Jessica laughed. "After seeing all those sexy things, the big question is whether after this weekend you'll forget it."

* * *

Durango turned around the moment he felt Savannah's presence in the wedding chapel. Immediately his breath caught at the sight of how strikingly beautiful she looked in her dress. It was perfect. Typically you couldn't improve on perfection, but in Savannah's case she had by adding the string of pearls around her neck, as well as with the way her hair shimmered like a silk curtain around her face, making her hazel eyes that much more profound. She was a vision straight out of any man's fantasy.

"Your bride is a beautiful woman, Rango. I'm not sure that's a good sign."

Durango arched an eyebrow and switched his gaze from Savannah to the man standing by his side, who'd leaned closer to whisper in his ear. McKinnon Quinn was the only person to whom he had told the real reason he was getting married, although he was sure Chase knew, as well. "Somehow I'll deal with it, McKinnon."

McKinnon chuckled. "I'm glad it's you who'll be doing the dealing and not me. A woman that beautiful might cause me to have a few weak moments."

Durango hoped like hell that he would be a stronger man than McKinnon when and if those moments occurred. He glanced over at Chase and Ian, wondering if they had the same thoughts as McKinnon since they had shifted their gazes from Savannah to stare at him.

A few moments later Durango was standing beside Savannah as they faced the older man who was employed by the Cascade to perform wedding ceremonies. Durango had no problem saying *I do* to any of the things the man asked him since he planned to adhere to his marriage vows for the brief time the marriage lasted.

Although he had been fully aware of each and every question he'd been asked, he'd also been fully aware of the woman standing beside him. The subtle scent of her perfume was zapping his senses. She could arouse feelings in him that were better left alone. And today of all days, the flesh beneath his suit was burning with memories of the time they had spent in the hot tub together.

"I now pronounce you man and wife. You may kiss your bride."

The man's words intruded on Durango's thoughts, giving him a mental start at the realization that the ceremony was over. He was now a married man and it was time to seal his vows with the traditional kiss. He turned to Savannah and saw her tense although she gave him a small smile.

At that moment he wanted to assure her that everything was going to be all right and they had done the right thing for their child. He reached out and touched her, gently ran the backs of his knuckles down her cheek while looking deeply into her eyes. And within seconds he felt her relax.

When a sigh of contentment eased from her lips he leaned forward. The kiss he'd intended was to be brief and light. But the moment his mouth touched hers, a strong sense of desire overtook him and he kissed her with a force that surprised even him.

His common sense told him that now was not the time for such a strong display of passion, but slipping his tongue into her mouth, wrapping his arms around her small waist and hungrily mating his mouth with hers seemed as natural as breathing. And the feel of her palms gliding over his shoulders wasn't helping one iota.

It was only when McKinnon touched his shoulder

and jokingly said aloud, "I see these two are off to a good start," that Durango pulled back.

"I'd rather the two of you not mention anything to the family about my marriage just yet," Durango said to Ian and Chase a few minutes after the ceremony had ended and he could speak with them privately. "I want to be the one to tell them."

Both men nodded. Then Ian said, "Mom isn't going to be happy about not being here at your wedding."

"Yes, but this is the way Savannah and I wanted to do things."

"When are you going to tell everyone?" Chase inquired. It wasn't easy keeping secrets in the Westmoreland family.

"I'm going to call the folks when we get back. Once I tell Mom, the news will spread like wildfire. But it will be another month before we'll be able to travel home. One of the rangers is out on medical leave and we're shorthanded."

"When you do come home expect Aunt Sarah to have one hell of a wedding reception planned," Chase said, grinning. "She might be upset at first about your elopement, but she'll be ecstatic that another one of her sons has gotten married."

Durango nodded, knowing that was the truth. "I don't have a problem with her planning a reception," he said, thinking his mother was going to be surprised when she did see Savannah because she'd be showing a little by then. Then Sarah Westmoreland would be happy for two reasons. Another one of her sons would have married and she would have her first grandchild on the way.

"Your bride is on her way over here to claim you for more pictures," Ian said, grinning since he had been the one to hire a private photographer for the occasion. He wanted to have lots of pictures for his mother once she found out about the quickie wedding. Although Durango hadn't told him why he and Savannah had eloped, Ian thought he knew his brother well enough to know there was only one reason why a devout bachelor like Durango would have gotten married. Time would tell if his assumption was true.

"Savannah is a beautiful woman," Ian said, pretty sure his brother already knew it.

"She is, isn't she?" Durango agreed as he watched Savannah cross the room.

"You're a lucky man," Ian decided to add for good measure.

Durango continued to watch as Savannah came closer and at that moment he couldn't help but think the very same.

An hour or so later Savannah was stepping out of the shower. She glanced around the bathroom and noticed that the spa-style bathtub was large enough to accommodate at least four people.

She couldn't help wondering what Durango was doing. After sharing a wedding dinner with Ian, Chase and Jessica, they had returned to their suite, said goodnight and gone to separate bedrooms.

A part of her was disappointed that he hadn't kissed her goodnight. But she knew the reason why he hadn't. One kiss would lead to another, then another and eventually to something neither of them could handle. Durango was intent on keeping his word to keep his distance and she appreciated him for doing so.

He had looked so darn good at the ceremony that for one tantalizing moment she had wished that their wedding was real. But she knew that wasn't possible. In about a year or so, he would be going his way and she would be going hers. After all, they were sharing an in-name-only marriage.

But still…

Would having Durango for a temporary lover be so bad? It was amazing how you could develop an all-consuming craving for something you were perfectly fine doing without only months before. Prior to her one night with Durango she'd dated, but had never been into casual sex. She hadn't been involved with anyone since she'd broken up with Thomas Crawford and she hadn't felt as if she was missing out. But all of that changed the night she and Durango had conceived their baby. From that night on she had been acutely aware of her body and its needs.

And then there were the memories that wouldn't go away. Durango and their night together had definitely left her with some lasting, vivid ones and a particularly special little moment, she thought, affectionately rubbing her tummy.

She glanced over at the bed and looked at the gown she intended to sleep in tonight. Alone. If she decided to share an intimate relationship with Durango, she had to remember that it would be with no strings attached. He didn't love her and she didn't love him. Remembering that would definitely make things easier emotionally when the time came for them to part ways.

She crossed the room and picked up the low-cut, short, barely there, flesh-tone nightgown and thought about the kiss they had shared after the man had announced them man and wife. She could still feel the heat from his lips on hers and just thinking about that kiss and the one they had shared last night in the hot tub sent shudders racing through her body. There was something about Durango Westmoreland that just kept her blood heated. Jessica had been right. Westmorelands weren't ordinary men.

Durango had been right, as well. There was no way they could entertain the thought of being married—even on a short-term basis—without there ever being a chance of them sharing a bed. She could see that now. Some marriages could truly be in *name* only, but she realized now that theirs would have to be in *bed* and *name* only. And she could handle that because once the marriage ended, she would begin living a solitary life. Her total concentration would be on raising her child. She wouldn't have time to become involved with a man. To be perfectly honest, it wouldn't matter to her if she never had another lover. Her affair with Durango would be enough to sustain her.

She knew what he said about abiding by her decision until she indicated she wanted things to be different between them. Well, now she had decided. She wanted things to be different.

Savannah saw Durango the moment she stepped out of the bedroom. He was standing on the balcony, gazing out at the lake. His chest was bare and he was wearing a pair of black silk pajama bottoms. His broad muscled chest and shoulders seemed to catch the remnants of the fading sunlight and it gave his dark skin an even richer glow. She wished she had time to get her camera and capture him on film so she could always have the breath-taking image at her fingertips.

As she continued to watch him her heartbeat quickened and the heat he had deliberately turned up earlier with his kiss was inching its way into a flame as she felt her body respond to his mere existence. And then, as if he'd sensed her presence, he turned slowly, capturing her eyes with his.

They stood there for a moment, separated by a few feet while sexual tension flowed between them the same way it had that night in Atlanta, and Savannah could feel herself slowly melting beneath the heat of Durango's intense stare.

And then he moved, slowly closing the distance separating them, soundless as his bare feet touched the carpeted floor. She wondered if he knew the effect he was having on her, or if he knew just how beautiful he was.

Usually one didn't think of a man as beautiful, but in this case she had to disagree. Durango Westmoreland was handsome, good-looking and devastating. But he was also beautiful in a manly sort of way. It was there in the shape of his face, the intensity of his dark eyes, the build of his high cheekbones and the fullness of his lips. The closer he got to her, the more her body responded and she braced herself for the full impact when he came to a stop in front of her. He glanced down at her outfit and then met her gaze. She saw the questions in his eyes and felt the heat in them, as well.

"I've changed my mind about a couple of things," she said softly, thinking how good he smelled.

"Have you?"

She met his gaze levelly. "Yes."

"And what have you changed your mind about?" he asked in a voice that Savannah thought sounded way too sexy.

"About my wedding night."

His eyebrows lifted. "*Your* wedding night?"

"Yes, I've decided that I want one."

He studied her. His gaze dark and heated. "Do you?"

"Yes." She was fully aware that he knew what she meant, but because he hadn't wanted to risk a misunderstanding, he had to be absolutely sure.

"Okay, I can handle that. Is there anything else that you want?"

She bit her lip a few times before saying, "I want for us to share a bed during the time we're married. I think we're mature enough to handle it, don't you?"

For a minute he seemed to absorb her words in silence before allowing a smile to touch his lips. "Sure, I don't see any problem in that. Do you mind telling me what made you change your mind?"

"I think it would be hard for us to share a house without sharing a bed. We're too attracted to each other and…"

He arched an eyebrow when she didn't finish. "And what?"

A smile touched the corners of her lips. "And I don't handle temptation very well, especially the Durango Westmoreland kind."

He reached out and placed his hand on her waist and

leaned forward slightly. "Can I let you in on a little secret?" he whispered against her lips.

"Sure."

"I don't handle temptation well, either. Especially the Savannah Claiborne kind, so I guess on some things we see eye to eye. That's a good sign."

"Is it?" She couldn't help but look at his mouth since it was so close to hers.

"Mmm, let me show you just how good it is."

And then he captured her lips and the moment he did so a wave of desire swept across her to settle in the pit of her stomach. He wrapped her tight into his arms and the intensity of the kiss made her bones melt. Moments later he reluctantly released her mouth.

"There is something I want to do, Savannah, and it's something I had intended to do at Chase and Jessica's wedding reception but never got around to doing," he said as his lips gently kissed the corners of her mouth and slowly moved to the side of her ear.

"What?" she asked softly, barely able to get the question out.

"Dance with you," he murmured in a low, sexy voice. He took a step back and held his hand out to her.

It was then that she heard the music, a melodic, soulful ballad by Anita Baker. The slow-tempo, easy-going jazzy sound of a saxophone in the background began flowing through her, touching all her senses, revving every nerve in her body and turning the heat up a notch more. Anticipation surged through her veins when she placed her hand in his.

Her pulse quickened when he pulled her closer into his arms, and she came into contact with his bare chest.

"Enjoy the dance," he said, his voice a sensuous whisper against her ear. He pulled her even closer and she knew the exact moment he dropped a kiss on the top of her head. Their bodies meshed together perfectly as they moved to the slow beat, making them fully conscious of the scanty clothing they were wearing. She could feel the heat deepening between them, and the way her flimsy negligee was clinging to her, shifting, parting with every movement of her body against his, she was certain he was aware of it, which only made her more aware of him. Especially the thick hardness of him that was pressed against her stomach.

Sighing deeply, she buried her face into his bare shoulder, absorbing his strength, his scent, the hard masculine feel of him. And as if on instinct, she gently licked his skin with her tongue. She knew he felt it when his arms tightened around her waist.

"If you lick me I get to lick you back," he murmured gently. "And in a place of my own choosing," he said in a low, sexy voice.

Savannah lifted her head and their eyes met, held. Deep down she anticipated and hungered for his next move, knowing it would be another kiss. And when he stopped moving and slowly lowered his head to hers, an urgent need took hold of her senses once again.

A mixture of need, greed and unadulterated longing flowed through her veins the moment their lips touched. His mouth fastened tight on hers and she instinctively absorbed everything there was about him. His tongue was unbelievably skillful when it came to giving her pleasure. It was like a magnet, clinging to whatever was in its path, attracting her own tongue, taking hold of it, dominating it, eliciting pressure, giving energy.

She heard herself whimper, while shiver after sensuous shiver coursed through her body. She was helpless to do anything but return the kiss with equal intensity while his body strained against hers.

And then she felt herself being lifted effortlessly into his arms and at that moment she knew that this was just the beginning.

Durango broke off the kiss the moment he placed Savannah on the huge bed in the bedroom she had chosen. Then he stood back and gazed down at her. Her negligee was feminine and enticing. Seeing her in it nearly sucked the very breath from his lungs.

Coming back to the bed he placed a knee on the pillow-top mattress and reached out and touched her breasts through the flimsy material. She made a low, sensuous sound the moment his hand came in contact with her and his fingers moved slowly, tracing a path around her nipples, feeling them harden beneath his fingertips.

His hand then slid down to her stomach. The flesh was exposed from the design of her lingerie, and he touched her bare skin, made circles around her navel, massaging it, caressing it, feeling the way her muscles tightened beneath his hand. Knowing his self-control was slipping, in one smooth sweep he removed the negligee completely, leaving her totally naked.

For the second time that night he actually felt the air he was breathing being sucked from his lungs. No woman, he quickly decided, should have a body this beautiful, this tempting, this seductive.

A slow, throbbing ache began inching its way through every part of him and as he stared at Savannah he felt an intense desire to possess her. Wanting to be sure she was ready for him, he reached out and touched the area between her legs, dipped his finger inside of her, stroked her, and saw she was indeed ready for him. She made a low moaning sound and he ceased what he was doing just long enough to remove his pajama bottoms.

"Durango."

His name was a whispered purr from her lips and he knew he was going to make love to her and not just have sex with her. The impact of that almost sent his mind spinning, but he refused to dwell on it now. He was too engrossed in how Savannah was making him feel and how his body was responding to the very essence of her. He was experiencing emotions he had not felt since the last time he had been with her. Nothing and he meant nothing would stop him from sharing this night with the woman who was now his wife.

Easing back on the bed with her, he kissed her, discovering again the sweetness that always awaited him in her mouth. And then he covered her body with his, lifted her hips and broke off the kiss to look deep into her eyes. He slowly entered her. The impact of their joining was so profound his body momentarily went still as their gazes locked.

"I know this might sound arrogant," he said in a low, husky tone. "But I think this," he said, pushing deeper into her body, "was made just for me."

Savannah smiled, adjusting her body to the intimate fit of his. "If you really believe that then who am I to argue? You definitely won't hear a peep out of me."

A sexy, amused chuckle rumpled from his lips. "Let's just see about that because I like the noises you make," he said, remembering the sounds she had made the last time they had come together.

He began moving, a slow pace, needing to feel himself thrusting deep inside her, needing to arouse even further that feminine hunger within her that he longed to release. He wanted to stir it up, whisk it to a level it had never been before and then give her what they both needed. He wanted her hungry for him, starving for him, desperate for him.

Durango refused to let her hold back on anything with him, especially his need to become one with her. His desire became even more feverish from the rhythmic movements of Savannah's hips.

He wanted it all and more than anything he needed to hear her express her satisfaction. And with that goal in mind, he continued to move against her, sliding back and forth, stroking in and out between her legs, letting her feel the workings of his solid shaft within her as his hand lifted her hips for better contact, more intense pleasure. Several times his body nearly shuddered with the force of his own release but he found the strength to hold back, keep himself in check.

But the moment Savannah cried out in ecstasy, and he felt her body tighten around his, using every feminine muscle she possessed to aggressively claim what she wanted, he gave in and succumbed to his powerful release that pushed him over the edge.

And when he leaned down and captured her mouth, clung to it, devoured it like a starving man, he tightened his arms and legs around her, tilted her body at an angle that would increase their pleasure. Durango knew at that moment if he lived to be a hundred years old, he would only find this degree of pleasure here, in Savannah's arms.

He was forced to admit that only with this woman could he claim complete sexual fulfillment. Only with her.

Ten

Durango shook his head as he raised his eyes to the ceiling. He and Savannah had returned to his ranch that morning and he had decided to wait until late afternoon to make the call to his family.

"Yes, Mom, I'm telling you the truth. I got married on Friday, and yes, I married Jessica's sister, Savannah."

He gazed across the room at Savannah, who was walking out of the bathroom. She had just showered and was wearing a beautiful blue silk bathrobe. A towel was wrapped around her head because she'd also washed her hair.

"Mom, Savannah and I eloped and got married in Lake Tahoe. Ian knew about it but I swore him to secrecy, so he was right not to tell you."

He nodded moments later. "Yes, it's okay for you and Savannah's mom to get together and plan a reception, but I'll have to get back to you and let you know when we can come to Atlanta. It won't be for another three to four weeks."

After a few moments of nodding, he then said, "Savannah and I met at Chase's wedding, fell in love and decided to get married quietly. Without any hoopla," he tacked on, borrowing Savannah's words.

He turned and watched as she removed the towel from her head, and he saw how the mass of dark, curly hair tumbled around her shoulders. He watched as she lifted her arms and began drying her hair. Doing so stretched her silk robe, showing off her generous curves. There was something about watching her dry her hair that was a total turn-on. He hoped it had nothing to do with the fact that this was his bedroom and she looked so damn good in it. Even her clothes that were hanging next to his in the closet looked right.

He frowned, not liking the thought of that. And then he cleared his throat, trying to concentrate on what his mother was saying. "Yes, Mom, you can tell the rest of the family, and yes, Savannah is here. Would you like to speak with her?" he asked, eager to get off the phone.

He could last only so long under his mother's intense inquisition. Just like Ian had said, their mother had been angry at first, but the news that another of her sons had married had smoothed her ruffled feathers. And it amused him that already she had her sights on the next of her sons who she felt was ready for matrimony. He chuckled, thinking Ian, Spencer, Quade and Reggie had better watch out.

"Okay, Mom, and I love you, too. Give Dad my best. Now here's Savannah."

"Be prepared," he whispered, before handing her the phone.

He then watched and listened while Savannah began talking to his mother. She first apologized, and accepted all blame for their decision to elope. Then told Sarah Westmoreland in an excited voice that she would love for her to plan a reception, and agreed with the older woman that it would be a wonderful idea to get Savannah's mother involved, too.

Durango was about to walk out of the room when Savannah promised to send his mother digital pictures taken at the wedding. Sending pictures was a nice touch that was sure to win Savannah brownie points with his mom.

When Durango returned twenty minutes later after taking a shower, Savannah was still on the phone with his mother. He gave Savannah an apologetic smile as he sat on the bed beside her. After another ten minutes he'd had enough and surprised Savannah by taking the phone out of her hand.

"Mom, I think you've talked to my wife long enough. It's our bedtime. We're newlyweds, remember?"

"Durango!"

He placed a finger to his lips, prompting Savannah to silence. "Thanks, Mom, for understanding. And yes, I'll make sure Savannah sends those photos to you tonight before she…ahh, goes to sleep. Good night, Mom." He chuckled as he quickly hung up the phone.

Savannah glared at him. "Durango Westmoreland, how could you embarrass me that way by insinuating that we—"

He kissed her mouth shut and then tugged her backward on the bed, removing her robe in the process. "I didn't imply anything that isn't true," he said, after releasing her lips.

He kissed her again, then pulled back and said, "Mmm, this is how I like you—naked and submissive." He knew his words would definitely get a rise out of her.

She pushed against his chest. "And just who do you think is submissive? I want you to know that…"

He kissed her again, thinking how dull his life had been before she came into it. Then just as quickly he decided that kind of thinking sounded like he was getting attached—and he didn't do attachments. But then again, he had to be honest enough and admit that for a man who'd always liked his privacy, he was thoroughly enjoying having Savannah around…even if she would only be there on a temporary basis.

When he finally released her mouth, she looked at him as desire darkened her eyes and said softly, "You aren't playing fair."

He met her gaze with an intensity he felt all the way to his toes and said hoarsely, "Sweetheart, I'm not playing at all."

Durango then stripped off his robe and stretched his naked body out beside her, pulling her into his arms and kissing her again. When he finally broke off the kiss he smiled down at her. "So, did you enjoy our trip to Lake Tahoe?"

She reached up and ran her fingers through the hairs on his chest, thinking about all the things they had done together, especially the time they had spent in bed. Durango, she had discovered, had extraordinary stamina. "Yes," she finally said, thinking just how much she had liked spending time at the Rolling Cascade with him. "It was a very rewarding experience."

"And you didn't once have morning sickness," he pointed out.

She grinned. "And I did enjoy the break. Maybe this bracelet works after all."

He lifted her hand and kissed her wrist. Then he smoothed his hands over her stomach, massaging gently, liking the thought that his child rested there. "And I take it our baby is well?"

"Yes, she's doing just fine."

"That's good to know. Now I can turn my full attention to the mother." He whispered the words in her ear and the sound was so low and seductive that it made every muscle in her body quiver.

"And how will you do that?" she asked innocently, knowing the answer but wanting him to expound anyway.

"I can show you better than I can tell you."

Cocking her head, and with a seductive glint in the depths of her hazel eyes, she said, "Then show me."

And he did that night. Numerous times.

"That's it. Move a little to the right. Oooh, yes. Now tilt your head a little back. Just a little. That's perfect, now hold it right there."

It was at that moment that Savannah took Durango's picture, just one of several she had taken already that day after he'd come in from work. She had convinced him that she needed to use up the rest of her film and that he would make the perfect model.

"Now open your shirt and let me see your chest."

He frowned. "Hey, just what kinds of photos are you taking?"

She grinned. "I told you. I want to sell my boss on the idea of doing a calendar on park rangers. They do them on firemen and policemen all the time. It's about time we honor American heroes."

He crossed his hand over his chest, ignoring the fact that Savannah and her camera were still clicking. "And just who will be buying these calendars?" he asked, thinking about a calendar that his cousin Thorn had done for charity a couple of years ago. They had sold like hotcakes.

She chuckled. "Anyone who appreciates good art… as well as a good-looking man. Besides, I think it would be a great idea for a charity fund-raiser. I can see you as Mr. February."

He lifted a brow. "Why Mr. February?"

She shrugged, and then said, "I think of you as Mr. February because that's the month this is, and so far it's been a good one—morning sickness and all. Also, February makes you think of hearts, and it was this month I heard a heart…the one belonging to our baby… so, you being Mr. February makes sense even if what I just said doesn't."

Durango looked at her with understanding because to him everything she said *did* make sense. No matter how long their marriage lasted or when it ended, the month of February would always have a special meaning to them. Without saying anything else he undid the top button while she snapped away with her camera.

"Sexy. Yes, that was one sexy pose," she said, looking up at him, deciding she'd taken enough pictures of him for now. Just then her pulse quickened due to the totally male look he was giving her.

"You think so?"

"Yes," she said, unzipping the case to put her camera in.

"I have to admit it was fun. When did you decide to get into photography?" he asked, leaning against the wooden rail of the outside deck.

Savannah glanced up at him. A great expanse of mountain range was in the background and for a heart-beat of a minute she was tempted to pull her camera out again. He was giving her another sexy pose.

"When I was a teen…sixteen, I think," she said. "My grandparents bought me my first camera and I drove everybody crazy with it by taking pictures whether I had their permission or not. I caught Mom, Rico and Jessica in some very embarrassing moments."

"Um, should I be worried?" he asked, grinning.

Savannah laughed. "No, I've grown up a lot since that time. Now I'm harmless."

Harmless? Durango wasn't so sure about that. Since Savannah had come into his life, nothing had been the same. The people he worked with couldn't believe it when he'd made the announcement that morning that he had gotten married. A number of them thought he was joking until Savannah had shown up at the ranger station at noon for their lunch date. Then he'd seen both under-standing and envy in a lot of the guys' eyes. He wondered what those same coworkers would think a year from now when he and Savannah went their separate ways.

"I hope you like what I cooked for dinner."

Savannah's words intruded, reclaiming his thoughts.

"I'm sure I will. But you didn't have to go to any trouble. I could have fixed something when I got in."

She laughed. "It's the least I can do while you're at work every day. I'm not used to being home all day. In fact, I pitched the calendar idea to my boss. If he approves the project, I'll be busy. Do you think your co-workers will mind having their pictures taken?"

Durango shook his head and grinned. "No, they'll probably get a kick out of it. The thought of being featured on a calendar will boost a few of their egos, I'm sure."

He studied her, sensing something was bothering her. He hadn't picked up on it earlier, but now without a camera in her hand it was becoming obvious. He couldn't help wondering if she oftentimes used her camera as an emotional shield.

"Did something happen today that I should know about, Savannah? Does it have anything to do with your mother or your brother?"

He knew her mother was still in Paris and Savannah had spoken to her the day before. She hadn't reached her brother until later in the day. He had been surprised but happy with her news and was looking forward to their visit to Philly.

Durango watched as she took a deep breath and said, "No, it's not about my family."

He nodded. That could only mean one thing. It was about *his*. "Did someone in my family call you today?"

"Yes."

"Who?"

He saw the small smile that touched her lips before she said, "It would probably be easier to ask who didn't. You have a rather large family."

Large and overwhelming, Durango thought, giving her his full attention. "And?"

"And…er…everyone, although surprised by the news we had gotten married, seemed genuinely sincere in wishing us the best, which made me feel like a phony."

He understood her ambivalence because he'd felt the same way at work today. "You're not a phony. Our decision to have a temporary marriage is our business and no one else's."

"Yes, I know…but."

He lifted an eyebrow. "But what?"

"But everyone was so nice. Even your cousin Delaney called all the way from the Middle East. And all the Westmoreland spouses, those married to your cousins and brother, called to welcome me into the family. They said from this day forward we would all be sisters. It was the same welcome Jessica told me they gave her. Do you know how that made me feel?"

She was staring at him with a strained expression on her face. He smiled at her. "No, how did that made you feel?"

"Special. I've always dreamed of belonging to a huge family, but it's not for real. Do you know what I'm saying? Am I making much sense?"

Yes, he knew what she was saying and she was making plenty of sense. He remembered that one of the main reasons she had agreed to marry him was that she wanted their child to have something she'd never had— a chance to belong to a large family; a family who would always be there for you through the good times or bad; a family who stuck together no matter what; a family that instilled strong values in future generations and a family who proved time and time again that when the going got tough, they didn't get going. They rallied around each other and gave their support.

"Yes, I understand," he said, after expelling a deep breath. "No matter what, there will always be a bond between us because of our child. You know that, don't you?"

"Yes, I know it, but I still feel like I'm being deceitful and that bothers me."

Not for the first time, Durango compared Savannah with Tricia. The more he did so, the more he was discovering there was no comparison. Both were city girls for sure, but where being deceitful actually bothered Savannah, Tricia hadn't shown any remorse when she'd looked him dead in the eyes and told him that she'd played him for a fool.

"I'm going to put dinner on the table now, Durango. I'll let you know when everything is ready."

Feeling her need to change the subject, he asked, "Need my help?"

"No. I can manage."

Moments after Savannah left, Durango turned to gaze out at the mountains. Today was a clear winter day and what he saw was breathtaking, a sight to behold, and it provided such a picturesque view that it made him appreciate his decision to settle down in these parts years ago.

He'd always found comfort in looking at the mountains when something weighed heavily on his mind and today Savannah was weighing heavily on his mind.

Although he had decided that Tricia's and Savannah's characters weren't anything alike, he still felt as though he was reliving the past. It had been so quick, too easy to fall in love with Tricia, and he had done so, proudly wearing his heart on his sleeve. But once she had ripped that sleeve, he had decided it could never be repaired. Under no circumstances would he allow himself to be that vulnerable again.

Durango knew the difference between lust and love and right now what he felt for Savannah was nothing more than lust. She had caught his eye from the first; they had made love, made a baby, and now they were married. But still the very thing that had drawn them together from the start was good old-fashioned lust. And they were taking it to a whole other level. Just the thought of what they had shared over the past few days made his breath catch, and last night, through the wee hours of the morning, had been the epitome of perfection.

He would be the first to admit that during one of those moments, a part of him had analyzed, fantasized, even had gone so far as to consider the idea of more than a year with her. But then that rip in his sleeve, that deep gash in his heart, had reminded him that there were some things in life that a man never got over. The pain he had suffered that one time had completely closed his mind to the prospect of ever loving again.

That's the way it was and that's the way it would stay.

Later that night Durango and Savannah sat cross-legged on the floor in front of the fireplace. They had eaten and showered and were ready to relax.

"Dinner tasted wonderful tonight, Savannah."

She smiled over at him. "Thanks. That's my grandmother's favorite dish," she said of the steak and baked potatoes she had prepared.

"So," Durango said, stretching out to lie on his side. "How do you suggest we spend the rest of the evening?"

She grinned at him and said teasingly, "I could take more pictures."

"I don't think so. Let's think of doing something else."

"Something like what?"

"Something like finding out just how hot things can get between us."

His words made her pulse quicken and she watched his mouth tilt into a very seductive smile. "Um, what do you have in mind?" she asked, meeting his gaze and holding it tight.

"Come here and let me show you," he said, reaching out and gently snagging her wrist to bring her on the floor beside him. She watched his every movement as he removed her robe. "Aren't you curious about the next step?" he asked.

She glanced down at his lap and saw the size of his arousal through his robe and immediately, her feminine muscles clenched in appreciation and anticipation. "No, I have an idea how this is going to get played out," she said, her breath almost catching in her throat.

"Good."

"But I do have one request," she said, wrapping her arms around his neck.

"What?"

"Let me take off your robe."

He smiled. "Go for it."

When she had removed his robe she took her tongue and licked a section of his shoulder before she drew back and looked at him. "You have a beautiful body."

He chuckled. "You think so?"

"Yes."

"Thanks, and I think you have a beautiful body, as well, and it's a body that I want to get all into."

"Well, in that case…"

He moved closer to her, growled low in his throat as he nudged her on her back. Like a leopard on the prowl, he cornered his prey and when he had her just where he wanted her he whispered softly, "Now it's my turn to lick."

And he did just that, starting with the insides of her thighs before moving to savor another part of her.

"Durango!"

Only when he was nearly intoxicated with the taste of her did he ease his body over hers to take her hard and fast, putting everything he had into each mind-wrenching thrust and watching her features glow with the pleasure he was giving her. And when he felt the quivering deep in her womb where his child nestled, he threw his head back and rocked furiously against her the same way she was rocking against him.

It pleased him immensely to know she was on fire, but only *for* him and *with* him. And when she arched against him and groaned from deep within her throat, he felt those same sensations that engulfed her rip through him as one hell of an orgasm slammed into him, lifting him to a place he'd never been before, pushing him high above the clouds, the earth, the entire universe.

And when he drove into her again and then again, he was met with an immense feeling of satisfaction. Knowing she was reaching the same level of mind-shattering pleasure as he was put him in total awe of everything they were sharing. He couldn't get enough of her. She was simply amazing. A city girl by day and a mountain wildcat by night.

And as she continued to pull everything out of him, take what he'd never given another female, he could only think of the remaining months they would be together and knew when she left, his life would never be the same.

"Get some rest, baby. I'm going to my office for a while," Durango whispered in Savannah's ear. After making love in front of the fireplace, he had picked her up in his arms to carry her into the bedroom and tucked her into bed. Quietly closing the door behind him, he went downstairs to his office.

He immediately walked over to the window. The moon's light cast a beautiful glow on the mountains, giving him a feeling of warmth, and for a while he stood there thinking that things couldn't get any better than this. He loved where he lived, he enjoyed his job and for a short while he wasn't living alone.

Sharing dinner with Savannah had been wonderful and afterward they had showered together as if it was the most natural thing to do. But nothing could top the lovemaking that had come later. It seemed that each and every time they came together was better than the last, and that thought was beginning to bother him.

Deciding he didn't want to dwell on it any longer, he was about to take a seat behind his huge desk when the phone rang. So it wouldn't disturb Savannah, he quickly picked it up, not bothering to check caller ID as he normally did. "Hello."

"What the hell is going on, Durango?"

He leaned back in his chair, recognizing his oldest brother's voice immediately. "Jared. And how are things with you?"

"Cut the crap and answer my question."

Durango rolled his eyes. Jared, the attorney, was his no-nonsense brother. Marriage had softened him some, but he was still a hard case. "What makes you think something is going on?"

"You got married."

Durango smiled. Yes, that would say it all. "It was time, don't you think? You seemed happy, so I decided to try it."

"And you want me to believe that?"

"That would be nice."

"Well, I don't."

"Figures."

"And Ian isn't talking."

Durango smiled. "That's good."

"Mom's overjoyed, of course," Jared Westmoreland went on to say. "I think she e-mailed every single family member those pictures she got over the Internet."

"Okay, Ian's not talking, but Mom's happy, so what's your problem, Jared?"

"I want to know why you did it."

"The reason I told you earlier wasn't good enough?"

"No."

He wasn't surprised. Of his five brothers, it was Jared who knew him the best. He could never pull anything over the brother who was nearly three years older and to Durango's way of thinking, plenty wiser. Whereas other relatives would cautiously buy the story that he and Savannah had fabricated, he immediately thought of three members of the Westmoreland family who would not. Jared and his cousins Dare and Stone.

The attorney in Jared would put up an argument no matter what Durango said, and because Dare—the current sheriff of College Park, Georgia—was a former FBI agent, he had a tendency to be suspicious of just about everything.

And Durango dreaded the call he knew he would eventually get from his cousin Stone. He and Stone were only months apart in age and had always been close. Durango figured the only reason Stone hadn't called yet to give him hell was because he and his wife, Madison, were somewhere in Europe on a book promotion tour.

"Are you going to tell me what I want to know, or will I have to take drastic measures and start an investigation?" Jared asked, breaking into Durango's thoughts.

"Um, what drastic measures would those be?"

"How does catching the next plane to Montana to check out things for myself sound?"

Not too good. Durango sighed, knowing Jared was dead serious and because of that he decided to come clean. "Savannah is pregnant."

He heard his brother's deep sigh. Then for a few moments Jared was silent, evidently taking it all in.

"How far along?" Jared finally asked.

"Going into her third month."

Silence again. Then Jared said, "It happened Christmas night."

Durango lifted an eyebrow. "How did you know?"

"For Pete's sake, Durango, do you think you weren't missed at the card game that night? Hell, we'd all been counting on winning all your money. And besides that,

I couldn't help but notice you were attracted to the woman and we all saw you leave the reception to walk her to her room."

Durango smiled, remembering. "You all saw too much that night."

"Whatever." Then moments later Jared asked, "The two of you made a decision to get married for the baby's sake?"

"Yeah, that just about sums it up. But our marriage is only temporary."

"Temporary?"

"Yes, until the baby is around six months old. I didn't want my child born illegitimate and I wanted to be around during Savannah's pregnancy to bond with it and spend some time with them for a while afterward."

"And what happens after that?"

"Then we part ways. But Savannah and I have agreed to always be there for the baby. She knows I want to be a part of its life and Savannah wants that, too. It won't be easy with us living so far apart, but we'll manage."

There was another long pause and then Jared asked, "And you're okay with the temporary setup?"

Durango frowned. "Why wouldn't I be?"

"I saw those pictures Mom is so proudly brandishing about town. At your wedding, you and Savannah looked good together, actually happy. If I didn't know better, then I—"

"But you do know better, which is why you made this call. Don't let those pictures fool you, Jared. The only thing going on between the two of us is the baby. Six months after it's born Savannah will go her way and I'll go mine."

"And until then the two of you will live together happily as man and wife?"

"More or less." And at the moment he was thinking more because he was discovering that Savannah was such a giving person, he couldn't imagine her giving less.

"Be careful, Durango."

Durango's eyebrow lifted higher. "Be careful of what?"

"Discovering the fact that your heart isn't really made of stone and that it might be putty in the right woman's hands."

Durango frowned. "Trust me, it won't happen to me."

Jared laughed. "I thought the same thing. Although I'm not complaining now, mind you. I discovered the hard way that the worst types of affairs are the pretended kind."

"What are you talking about?"

There was another pause and Durango thought he heard the sound of his brother sipping something. Probably a glass of the finest wine. He could imagine Jared doing so in that million-dollar home he owned. Jared was a hotshot Atlanta attorney who over the years had made a name for himself by handling high-profile cases involving celebrity clients. Up until a year ago, Jared had been determined to stay a bachelor like Durango, and then Dana Rollins happened, surprising the hell out of everyone in the Westmoreland family who'd known Jared's stand on marriage. He'd always claimed it wasn't for him. He was a divorce attorney who ended marriages, not put them together. But now he was a happily married man who didn't care if the world knew how much he loved his wife.

"My engagement to Dana," Jared finally said, pulling

Durango's thoughts to the present then tumbling them back to the past when he remembered Jared's surprised announcement of his engagement at their father's birthday party last Easter.

"What about your engagement?"

"There never was one, at least not a real one."

Durango frowned, wondering what the hell his brother was saying. He was too tired, not in the right frame of mind to try to figure out anything tonight. "What do you mean there never was one? I was there when you announced it."

"I never announced anything. Mom did."

Jared's words made him think. Jared was right. Their mother had been the one who'd made a big fuss about Jared's engagement. Jared hadn't really said much. But then he hadn't spoken up to deny it, either.

"Are you saying you went along with an engagement because Mom put you on the spot?"

"There was more to it than that, Durango. If you recall, soon after that we found out about that lump in Mom's breast. She'd made it up in her mind I was getting married and the last thing I wanted to do was to burst her bubble, considering everything."

Durango nodded. "So you pretended an engagement? And you actually got Dana to go along with doing something like that?"

"Yes, but in the midst of it all we fell in love."

Durango shook his head, thinking how his brother had effectively pulled the wool over their eyes. "Who else knew the truth?"

"Dare. No one else needed to know. The only reason I'm even telling you is that I want you to see how things can happen."

"Things like what?"

"How you can enter into a situation thinking one way and in the end, your thinking can change. The more I got to know Dana and spent time with her, the more I wanted more out of our relationship. I saw Savannah that night and I sensed the attraction between the two of you. She's a woman a man can easily fall in love with. I could see that happening to you."

Durango sat up straight in his chair. "Well, I can't," he snapped. "I'm happy things turned out that way for you and Dana, but it won't for me and Savannah."

"Can you be sure of that?"

"Yes, I can be sure. You were evidently capable of loving someone. I'm not. At least not now. If I had met Savannah before Tricia, then I —"

"When will you let go of what she did to you?"

"I have let go, but that doesn't mean I want to open myself up to the same kind of hurt again."

"And you think that you will be?"

"I'm thinking that I'm not willing to take the risk."

"And what about Savannah?"

"What about her?"

"What if she feels differently?"

"She doesn't and she won't. She was more against us marrying than I was. In fact, I had to convince her it was the right thing to do. She only agreed to do it for the baby's sake. She'll stay for six months and then she's out of here."

"And the two of you have agreed to all of this?"

Durango rolled his eyes. "Yes, but we haven't put it in writing, if that's what that attorney's mind of yours is driving at. Hey, maybe that isn't such a bad idea. I want her to know I will continue to do right by her even after the baby is born. Draw me up something, will you?"

"Draw you up what?"

"I don't know. Some legal document that spells out that I will continue to support her and the baby after the time is up. I want to set up a college fund and I intend to provide generous monthly allotments for my child, which I'll be able to afford thanks to that business venture I'm in with McKinnon."

"Are you sure you want to bring a legal document into the picture now?"

"Why not? I'd think she would appreciate knowing I will support her, something her father didn't. She has this thing about how her old man treated her pregnant mother when they got married and he never did right by her, Jessica and her brother. I want to assure Savannah that I have no intentions of treating her that way."

A half hour later Durango ended the call with Jared after telling him everything he wanted to put in the document. Whether his brother wanted to accept it or not, his marriage to Savannah was only temporary and Durango did not intend to ever forget that fact.

Eleven

The next two weeks were busy ones for Savannah. It helped tremendously that her bouts of morning sickness were infrequent and she woke each day seeing it as another adventure.

Her boss was excited about the idea of a calendar to commemorate Yellowstone National Park and the men who protected its boundaries. In addition to the calendar, he also envisioned something bigger and he had suggested a documentary film. She was excited about the idea and spent most of her days shooting footage that might be used for the project.

Her nights belonged to Durango. After dinner she would read to him from the baby book, keep him abreast of all the changes that were taking place within her body, and then they went to bed. Each night Durango did his own investigation, getting firsthand knowledge by going deep inside her body. And each time he entered her, after bringing her to a feverish pitch, she was fully aware that the private moments they shared would remain a part of her, even after they had parted ways. But then she realized that something had happened that she hadn't counted on.

She had fallen in love with Durango.

As she stood looking out the window, a part of her wondered at what point it had happened. Had it been just last night, when they had showered together and he had made love to her in such a beautiful way that had brought tears to her eyes? Or had it been last week, when he had taken her on a hike up the mountain, and they had stopped at the hunting cabin that he and McKinnon had built and had enjoyed the packed lunch he'd made for them. Or later, before coming back down the mountain, when they had enjoyed each other, making love outside near a beautiful stream under a beautiful Montana sky. She would always relish the tender, loving moments they shared and knew that deep down she would miss Durango.

She turned when she heard the phone ring, and quickly crossed the room, thinking it was Durango, but the caller ID indicated it was her brother, Rico, instead.

"Hello."

"I know, Savannah."

Savannah lifted a brow having an idea of what he knew. Evidently her mother had let something slip. "You know what?" she asked innocently.

"That you're pregnant."

Savannah smiled wryly. That was Rico for you. Straight to the point. "I had planned to tell you when I thought the time was right."

There was silence for a moment and then he asked, "Are you okay with it?"

Savannah chuckled. "I'm more than okay with it. I'm ecstatic. Of course, I wasn't at first because I was nervous and scared more than anything. Then I decided since I never planned to marry anyway, at least I'd have a baby. I always wanted one."

"But you *did* get married."

"Only for the baby."

"Which is something you swore you'd never do."

She sighed deeply. Leave it to Rico to remind her of that. "This is different. Durango and I went into this marriage with our eyes open. We want what's best for our child and we'll do whatever it takes to make sure that happens."

"Even if it means sentencing yourselves to a loveless marriage?"

"Yes, but in our case it will only be temporary. We've agreed to a divorce when the child is six months old."

"And you're okay with that?"

"Sure. Why wouldn't I be?" she asked simply.

"No reason, I guess. When are you coming home?"

She shrugged. "Not sure. I had thought of coming to Philly to check on things, but all my bills are paid up, so there's no rush. Besides, I like it out here."

"And your husband?"

"What about him?"

"How's he treating you?"

In all the right ways that a man should treat a woman. That very thought came to the tip of Savannah's tongue and she hesitated, thinking of just how true it was. Maybe it was because they knew that things between them were only temporary, but whatever the reason, she enjoyed every second, every moment she spent with Durango.

But then it would be easy for her to do so anyway, because she'd fallen in love with him, and could now admit that she had done so the first time she had seen him at Jessica and Chase's wedding.

"Savannah?"

"Durango is treating me well, so don't worry yourself by thinking anything different. He's a good man."

"He got you pregnant."

She heard the anger in Rico's voice. "And he wasn't in that bed alone, remember that," she replied tersely. "Nor did he have my hands tied behind my back. Remember that, too," she added. "I'm a big girl, Rico."

He chuckled. "And you'll be getting even bigger in the coming months."

She smiled, glad the tension between them had passed. "Yes, and multiple births run in the Westmoreland family. So we might be getting double."

"Finding out that you're pregnant and the possibility of you having twins. That's a lot for me to deal with, Savannah."

Her smile deepened. "But I'm more than certain that you will."

"It was really nice of your coworkers to give this party in our honor," Savannah whispered to Durango while glancing around the room. Beth Manning, one of the female park rangers, had contacted her at the beginning of the week to tell her of the rangers' plans to host a postwedding party for her and Durango.

At first Savannah had felt dishonest, but then, like Durango had said, the terms of their marriage were nobody's business.

"Yes, it was nice of them," he agreed, placing his arm around her shoulders to pull her closer to his side. They were at the home of Beth and her husband, Paul. Paul was a veterinarian in the area.

Savannah thought that Beth and Paul had a beautiful house that was located not far from Durango's ranch, on the other side of the mountains. Inside the decor was different from Durango's. Instead of it having two stories, the rooms were spacious and spread out on one level. And one side of the living room was a huge picture window that had no curtains, blinds or shades to block the beautiful panoramic view of the mountains.

Savannah had met most of the park rangers who worked with Durango when she had joined him for lunch one day, but this was the first chance she'd gotten to meet their spouses. Already she liked everyone. She thought they were genuinely friendly and appreciated them for making her feel welcome and at home.

Everyone had brought a covered dish and they were enjoying themselves, having a good time basking in the decent weather as well as the delicious food. One thing Savannah noticed was that Durango rarely left her side. He was always there, either holding her hand or placing his arms around her shoulders. She knew to everyone who observed them they appeared to be a very happy couple.

"Are the two of you ready to open the gifts now?" A smiling and exuberant blond-haired, blue-eyed Beth came up to them and asked.

Durango glanced at his watch. It was nearing midnight. "Now would be good. It's getting late."

"When did you ever care about time, Durango? I've known you since college and you've never been known to leave a party early," Beth's husband Paul came to join them and asked with twinkling green eyes and a charming smile.

"Oh, but he's a married man now, Paul," Beth reminded her husband, grinning. "We're seeing a new Durango Westmoreland."

Savannah could only imagine how the old Durango had been. She'd known the first moment she'd seen him that he was irresistible to women. Any man with his dark, striking good looks and strong, masculine body had to be. She wasn't naive to assume that before she'd met him he had lived a quiet life that hadn't included women. In fact, Jessica had been quick to tell her that he was a playboy and chances were once he regained his freedom he would revert to his womanizer ways.

A short while later she and Durango found themselves seated in chairs that were in the middle of a circle. Everyone else sat around them.

One by one Beth handed Savannah a gift that she excitedly opened. She and Durango received wineglasses, bath towels, plants, throw rugs and various other gifts. Durango had watched the happy enthusiasm on Savannah's face as she opened each present. But it was the huge, beautiful blue satin bedspread that had caught everyone's attention, including his.

The lower part of his body actually stirred when Savannah unwrapped it. Immediately, he could envision it on his bed with them buried beneath it while they made love. He met her gaze and knew she had had the same vision, and that made his body stir even more. Lucky for him that was the last gift that needed to be opened.

"I'm going to load everything in my truck and Savannah and I are going to call it a night," he said to everyone while glancing at his watch again. "It's officially Sunday morning."

Paul chuckled. "Nobody made you the time keeper, Durango, but I understand. I've been married four years longer than you have."

Savannah didn't know what to say other than thanks and good night to everyone once the guys had helped Durango load all the packages into his truck.

"I never thought I'd live to see the day that Durango Westmoreland fell so hard for a woman," Penny Washington, another park ranger, came and whispered in Savannah's ear. "The two of you look so happy together."

It was on the tip of Savannah's tongue to say that looks were deceiving, but then she changed her mind. She wasn't sure how Durango actually felt about being with her, but she could inwardly admit she was very happy being with him. And that, she thought, was beginning to be the root of a very serious problem. It was all fine and dandy when the two of them had wanted the same thing out of their marriage—no emotional ties. But now she loved him, and it was getting harder and harder to pretend otherwise.

"Ready?"

She glanced up and noticed Durango had come back inside the house. She saw the look in his eyes. She recognized it. She was becoming used to it. But still, that didn't stop the sensation of air being ripped right out of her lungs. Already she felt her entire body melting.

She cleared her throat. "Yes," she said.

"Wait a minute, Durango. You know how these types of gatherings are supposed to end. You have to kiss your bride for us," one of the rangers called out.

Durango smiled and hollered back, "Hey, that's no problem." And then he leaned down and kissed her in front of everyone, taking her mouth as passionately and as thoroughly as he'd done when they'd been alone. His kiss made her want and desire him…and love him even more. The cheers, catcalls and whistles went unnoticed. She was too busy drowning in the taste of the man who was her temporary husband.

Durango had only made it partway to the ranch when he couldn't take it any longer. Pulling his truck over to the side off the road, he cut off the ignition then, after unsnapping their seat belts, he reached across the seat and pulled Savannah into his arms. He needed another kiss.

Her lips parted instantly, eagerly. She was full of fire and heat and the more he devoured her mouth, the more she returned his passion.

He liked the sound of her whimpering in pleasure; he liked the feel of her wiggling in his lap, trying to get even closer; and he liked the scent of her scintillating perfume.

He reluctantly withdrew his mouth from hers. If he didn't stop now they would wind up making love in his truck and he didn't want that. He wanted a bed. "As soon as we get home I'm going to teach you a skill every woman should know."

A quick surge of heat rushed through Savannah at his words. "And what skill is that?"

He gently squeezed her nipples through her blouse and grinned ruefully. "You'll find out soon enough." He then placed her back in her seat and snapped her seat belt in place.

Sitting beside him the rest of the way to the ranch was torture for Savannah. He had turned her on and there was no way she could get turned off. In silence she glanced over at him. It was a moonless night but the glow from the SUV's console was all the light she needed to study his profile and note the intensity that lined his features. She quickly realized that he was as turned on as she was.

When they reached the ranch he brought the truck to a stop, got out, strode over to the passenger side, opened the door, unsnapped her seat belt and lifted her into his arms. Walking swiftly, he headed for the house.

"What about the gifts?" she asked, pressing her face into his chest, relishing the masculine scent of him.

"I'll unload everything tomorrow. There's no time tonight."

She smiled, thinking he was certainly making time for something. He opened the door and, after kicking it back shut with the heel of his boot, he carried her up the stairs to his bedroom.

She didn't have to wonder what would happen next.

Durango undressed her in record time and then proceeded to undress. Soon he had her on her back and purring like a cat.

He touched her everywhere, with his hands and then with his mouth, first tugging gently on her nipples, letting his tongue bathe them as he licked away. She heard herself moan, groan and whisper his name several times.

Her legs felt weak. Her body ached. And her mind was being blown to smithereens.

No man could touch her and make her feel the way Durango was making her feel. She was certain of it. He could stroke her desire and fill all of her needs and only with him could she give her entire being, and share the very essence of her soul. Her love.

At the thought of how much she loved him, a pulse began beating deep inside of her, close to her heart. And when his mouth released her breasts to move lower, she nearly stopped breathing.

He touched her intimately and her body responded immediately. Her back arched and her hips bucked the moment his fingers slipped inside of her. His fingers stroked her, expertly, seductively, intently, and moments later, when his mouth replaced his fingers, her entire body nearly jumped off the bed at the same time that a small, hoarse, gurgle of pleasure found its way up her throat. If she could be granted one wish for them, besides wanting a healthy baby, she wanted this. Him. For the rest of her life.

"You make me think crazy stuff, Savannah," he whispered when he covered her body with his own and swiftly entered her, making her breath catch. She wondered what crazy stuff he was thinking because he was making her think crazy stuff as well. And the craziest was that she didn't want their marriage to end. But she knew there was no permanent future for them. She loved him, but he didn't love her. But tonight, she wanted it all and if she couldn't have the real thing, then she would pretend.

They had made love plenty of times but something

about tonight was different. She felt it in his every stroke, his every thrust into her hot and responsive body. Whatever fever that was consuming him began consuming her, as well.

And she couldn't take it anymore.

A deep-rooted scream tore from her lips and she felt it, the smoothness of his engorged flesh as it jetted a hot thickness deep inside her, getting absorbed in her muscles, every hollow and every inch of her womb. And when he leaned down and kissed her, the urgency of that kiss melted her further. She knew if she lived to be a hundred, Durango was the only man who would ever have her heart.

A short while later, bathed in the room's soft lamplight, she exhaled a satiated sigh as he pulled her closer into his arms. He kissed her gently as one hand possessively cupped her breast. "I can't get enough of you," he whispered huskily.

She couldn't get enough of him, either, and knew she never would. "What skill did you want to show me?" she asked, barely able to get the words out.

He shifted on his back, lifted her, smiled and said, "Now I want you on top."

"Tell me about your brothers," she said, bending her head toward his and whispering against his lips. After several hours of practicing her new skills, she couldn't move an inch even if she needed to.

He wrapped his arms around her waist, keeping her there, on top of him with their bodies connected. "I guess you should know something about them as you'll get to see them soon. I found out today that I'll be able to take two weeks off now that Lonnie is back at work," he said.

"That means we can fly to Atlanta and Philly?"

"Yes, within a week's time."

She snuggled closer. "I met all your brothers at Chase and Jessica's wedding, but I don't know much about them and I want to be prepared."

"Okay, then let me prepare you," he said. "At thirty-eight, Jared is the oldest and the only one who's married. He's the attorney in the family. Next comes Spencer. He's only eleven months younger than Jared. He's a financial planner. I always admired his ability to keep both his profession and personal life from falling apart a few years ago when his fiancée drowned. He took Lynette's death hard, and I doubt to this day that he has fully recovered. Spence lives in California and is the CEO of a large financial firm there."

He looked at her and gave her his disarming smile and said, "I'm the third oldest and you know everything there's to know about me. But if there's more you think you need to know, then I rather show you than tell you."

"No, I think I have a pretty good idea of what you're all about," she said, determined not to be sidetracked. "What about the others?"

His smile widened to touch the corners of his lips. "Then there are the twins, Ian and Quade. They're thirty-three. You spent time with Ian at our wedding. He was seriously involved a few years ago with a woman who worked as a deputy for Dare, but they broke up. I don't know the reason they split, and as far as I know, he hasn't gotten serious about another woman since then."

He shifted their bodies and placed her on top of him. She felt his staff had grown as he entered her. She felt stretched, hot and ready. "My brother Quade works for the Secret Service. We barely know where he is most of the time, and when he comes home we know not to ask any questions. And last but not least, there is Reginald, whom we call Reggie. He'll be turning thirty later this year. He owns his own accounting firm in downtown Atlanta."

Savannah lifted her head. She had heard the love, the respect and the closeness in Durango's voice when he'd spoken of his brothers. "Now what about your—"

"I'm through talking for a while."

She raised an eyebrow. "Are you?"

"Yes."

She smiled. "So what would you like to do?"

He grinned and the sexual chemistry between them was immediate and powerful. "I'd like you to perfect that skill I taught you earlier."

Twelve

Durango woke up on Monday morning with an ache in his right knee. Although a glance out the window indicated a clear day he knew the ache was a sign that a snowstorm was coming.

Being careful not to wake Savannah he eased out the bed and went into the bathroom. The moment the door closed behind him he took a deep breath and met his dark gaze in the vanity mirror. Except for the remnants of sleep still clinging to his eyes, he looked the same. Okay, he admitted he did need a shave. But there was something going on inside him that he couldn't see. It was something he could feel and it was something the depth of which he had never felt before.

Not even for Tricia.

At the thought of the one woman who had caused him so much pain, he felt…nothing. Not that ache that used to surround his heart, nor the little reminders of the heartbreak that he had survived. What he felt now was an indescribable fulfillment, one that was new but welcome. It was a fulfillment that Savannah had given him. A warm feeling that she had miraculously placed in his heart.

In a short period of time, being around her, spending time with her and getting to know her, Savannah Claiborne had done something no other woman had been able to do. She had taken his heartache away. She had opened new doors for him, passionate doors, doors filled with trust, faith, hope and love.

Love.

That one word suddenly made him feel disoriented. But just as quickly, he came to the realization that he did love Savannah. He loved everything about her, including the baby she was carrying. And he wanted them both, here with him, and not just temporarily, but for always. He didn't want their marriage to end. Ever.

He sighed deeply, admitting that Jared had been right. His heart had been putty in the hands of the right woman.

Savannah's hands.

Now, the big question was, what was he going to do about it? He'd had a hard enough job selling her the idea of a temporary marriage; she would probably fight him tooth and nail if he brought up the idea of a permanent one. But he would. Tonight. If he had to he would catch her at one of her weakest moments.

He would do whatever it took to win Savannah's heart.

Savannah waited for the mail with excitement. Her boss had indicated that he would be sending the contract for her to sign for the proposal she had submitted for the calendar and documentary. Already, several of Durango's coworkers, eager to participate, had volunteered.

As she sat at the table and sipped her tea she thought about the phone calls she had gotten from Durango. He'd called twice to warn her about a snowstorm that was headed their way. In the second call, he had informed her that he wanted to talk with her about something important when he got home. Although he wouldn't go into any details, she could tell by the tone of his voice that whatever he wanted to discuss was serious.

She heard the mail truck pull up and quickly placed her teacup aside and grabbed her coat off the rack. As soon as she stepped outside, she felt the change in the weather.

After getting all the mail out of the mailbox, she quickly went back inside to the warmth. Tossing all the letters aside that were addressed to Durango, she came across two that were addressed to her.

The first was the one she'd been waiting for, from the company where she worked. The second, however, caused her to lift an eyebrow. It was a letter from Jared Westmoreland's law firm. Curious, she ripped into the letter Durango's brother had sent her and pulled out the legal-looking document.

Tears began forming in her eyes when she read it. In his ever efficient way, Durango was taking every precaution by reminding her of the terms of their agreement, as well as putting in writing what he intended to do for her and the baby after their marriage ended. The purpose of the paper she held in her hand was to remind her of their agreement. Their marriage was nothing more than a business arrangement.

She wondered if that was what he wanted to talk to her about when he got home. Had he detected the change in her? Had she not been able to hide the fact that she loved him? Maybe he wanted to get everything out in the open, and back into perspective? Was the document his way of letting her know he was beginning to feel smothered and wanted her to leave?

A sudden pain filled her heart and she knew she could never stay where she wasn't wanted...or loved. Her mother had remained in such a situation, but Savannah had vowed that she never would. Tossing the document on the table, she went into the bedroom to pack. If she was lucky, she would be able to catch a plane to Philadelphia before the bad weather set in.

She was going home.

Durango glanced up at his office door and saw Beth standing there. He smiled. He hadn't had a chance to thank her for hosting the party the past weekend.

Before he could open his mouth, she quickly said, "Paul just called and said that an SUV resembling yours passed him on the road."

Durango lifted an eyebrow and sat up straight in his chair and frowned. He had begun using one of the park's SUVs so that Savannah wouldn't be without transportation at the ranch. "And he thinks he saw my Durango?"

"He said it looked a lot like yours and that it was headed toward Bozeman. He was concerned with the storm coming in."

So was Durango. He had called Savannah twice earlier to tell her about the bad weather coming their way and she hadn't mentioned anything about going out. Why on earth would she drive to town?

"Maybe it wasn't your truck, but one that looked like yours."

Durango knew Beth was trying to keep him from worrying, but he was already reaching for the phone to call home. Most people around these parts knew his truck when they saw it because of the custom chrome rims.

He began to panic when no one answered the phone at his place. He then tried Savannah's cell phone. When he didn't get an answer he hung up the phone and glanced back at Beth, who had a worried look on her face. A snowstorm in Montana wasn't anything to play with and the thought of Savannah out in one wasn't good. He stood, already moving toward the door. "I'm out of here. I need to find Savannah before the storm hits."

"Call me when you do."

"I will." He tossed the words over his shoulder as he quickly left.

No need to panic now, Savannah told herself as she continued to drive although she could barely see the road through the snow. It seemed the huge flakes had begun coming all at once, blanketing everything, decreasing her sight to zero visibility.

Knowing it was no longer safe to move Durango's truck another foot, she pulled to the shoulder of the road and killed the engine. She reached into her purse for her cell phone and tried several times without success to reach Durango. Without the heat in the truck, she soon began to feel chilled. She reached for the blanket Durango kept under the seat. Savannah wrapped it around her shoulders, grateful for the warmth it provided, but knew it was only a temporary measure. She wasn't sure how long she could sit here like this, but she also knew to get out of the truck in this type of weather would be suicidal. She wasn't far from the ranch but she wasn't familiar enough with the area to venture out on foot. She decided to stay put.

The best thing to do would be to wait and turn on the engine for heat every so often. She hoped and prayed that the storm would let up or that someone would find her.

Durango drove the road that led from Bozeman to his ranch. Within eight miles of his home he spotted his truck on the side of the road. Pulling up beside it, he quickly got out of the Jeep, ignoring the snowflakes that clung to his face. His heart was beating rapidly as he ran to his SUV.

His heart leaped in his chest the moment he opened the door. Savannah was wrapped in his blanket and curled up on the seat. He reached out and touched her and the first thing he noticed was that she was cold as ice. The second thing he noticed was her overnight bag and camera case on the floor. *Where was she going? Why was she leaving?*

"Savannah? Baby, are you okay? What's going on?"

When she didn't respond he panicked. He pulled her gently into his arms, sheltering her face in his thick, fur-lined parka.

His first inclination was to get her to a hospital and fast. But that was a fifteen-mile trip. He was adequately trained in first aid and made a quick decision to get Savannah to a warm place.

Since they were close to the ranch, he decided to go there. Once at home he would call Trina. He had spoken to her earlier and knew she was at the Marshalls' place on a medical call. The Marshalls' baby had picked the day of what looked to be one of the biggest snowstorms of the year to be born on.

Trina would have to pass by his place on the way home. If she hadn't left already, he would have her stop at his ranch. As he slogged through the deep snow to the SUV, he couldn't help worrying about his wife and child.

He didn't know why she had tried leaving him, but now that he had found her, there was no way he would ever let her go.

"And you're sure Savannah and the baby are going to be all right, Trina?"

Trina motioned for them to step out in the hallway before she began speaking. "Yes, they are both doing fine. I checked the baby's heartbeat and it's as strong as ever. That's a tough kid the two of you are going to have."

Durango had nearly been a basket case when she'd arrived. Any assumption she'd had that the only reason he had gotten married was because Savannah was pregnant had gotten blown out the window, smothered in the snow. What she saw in Durango was a man who truly loved his wife.

Seeing that her words had relaxed him somewhat, Trina continued by saying, "You did the right thing by bringing her here and getting her warm. Giving her that tea really did the trick. But I'm glad you found her when you did. I don't want to think about what would have happened if you hadn't. She knew the risk of carbon monoxide poisoning which is why she hadn't kept the truck's heater running and I'm glad she didn't."

Durango nodded. He was glad, as well. "How long will she be sleeping?"

"For another couple of hours or so. Just let her rest," Trina said, slipping into her coat.

"Are you sure you want to go out in this? You can stay and wait for things to clear up."

Trina smiled. "Thanks, but I know my way around these parts pretty good. Have you forgotten that I grew up here? I only live a few miles away. I'll be fine. And I promise to call you when I get home."

Durango nodded, knowing there was nothing he could say to Patrina Foreman that would make her change her mind. Perry had always said that stubborn was her middle name. "Thanks for everything, Trina. How can I repay you?"

"You already have, Durango. From the day you moved into the area, you were always a true friend to me and Perry, and then, after I lost him, you, McKinnon, Beth and everyone else in these parts were there for me, giving me the shoulder I needed to cry on and helping me keep the ranch running. For that I will always be grateful."

She smiled and continued by saying, "Perry and I were married for five happy years, and my only regret is that we didn't have a child together. Then I would have something of his that would always be with me. But you have that, Durango. You got the best of both worlds. You have a wife you love and the child she is giving you. Take care of them both."

An hour or so later, Durango stood at the window, barely able to see the mountains for the snow. It was falling thicker and faster. At least Trina had called to let him know she had made it home and he was glad of that. He had also called the rangers' station to let everyone know Savannah was safe and doing fine.

He sighed deeply and lifted the document he held in his hand and reread it. It had included all the things he had told Jared he wanted in it, and now after reading it he could just imagine what Savannah had thought, what she had assumed after reading it herself. How would he ever convince her to stay now?

He glanced around the room. The house would be cold, empty and lifeless without Savannah there. No matter what he needed to do, get on his knees and beg if he had to, he refused to let the woman he loved walk out of his life.

Savannah forced her eyes open although she wasn't ready to end her dream just yet. In it Durango had just removed her clothes, had begun kissing her. But a sound made her come awake.

She glanced across the room, and there he was, the man she loved, kneeling in front of the fireplace, working the flames and keeping her warm. She breathed in deeply as pain clutched at her heart. She recalled packing, trying to make it to the airport before the storm hit. How had she gotten back here, to a place where she wasn't wanted? That agonizing question made her moan deep in her throat and it was then that Durango turned around and stared at her, holding her gaze with his and with a force that left her breathless.

She watched as he stood and slowly came over to the bed, his gaze still locked on hers. "You were leaving me," he said in a low, accusing tone. "You were actually leaving me."

Savannah sighed. Evidently he wasn't used to women leaving him and the thought of her abandoning him hurt his pride. "You didn't want me anymore," she said softly, not knowing what else to say. "I thought it would be best if I left."

"Did you think that I didn't want you anymore because of that document Jared sent?" When she didn't respond to his question quickly enough, he said, "You assumed the wrong thing, Mrs. Westmoreland."

Savannah blinked. In all the weeks they had married, he had never called her that, mainly because they'd both known the name was only temporary. So why was he calling her that now? "Did I?"

"Yes, you did. I thought having everything spelled out in a document was what you'd want. I guess I was wrong."

"It doesn't matter," she said softly, trying to hold back her tears.

He came and sat on the side of the bed and took her hand in his. "Yes, it does matter, Savannah. It matters a lot because you matter. You matter to me."

She shrugged, weakly. "The baby matters to you."

"Yes, and the baby matters to you, too. But you also matter to me. *You* matter because I love you."

She blinked again and those beautiful hazel eyes of hers stared at him with disbelief in their depth. He was determined to make her believe and accept him. "I do love you. It would be a waste of time to ask exactly when it happened, but since we have all the time in the world you can go ahead and ask me anyway," he said, smiling and stretching out beside her on the bed.

"When?" she asked, barely able to get the single word out.

He paused, as if searching for the right words. "I think it was when I arrived late at the rehearsal dinner and saw you standing there talking to Jessica. And when you looked up and met my gaze, something hit me. I assumed it was lust, but now I know it was love. Lust would not have driven me to have unprotected sex with any woman, tipsy or not, Savannah. But when we made love I was driven with an urgency I'd never felt before to be inside you and feel the full impact of exploding inside you."

He grinned. "Pill or no Pill, no wonder you got pregnant. Now when I think about it, it would have really surprised the hell out of me if you hadn't. I was hot that night and so were you. Mating the way we did was just a pregnancy waiting to happen. It wasn't intentional, but it was meant to be. And regardless of how you feel about me, I love you."

He shifted a little to get closer to her. "A few weeks ago, before we married, you asked why I had an aversion to city girls and I never gave you an answer. Maybe it's time that I did."

And then he spent the next twenty minutes or so telling her about Tricia, the one woman he'd actually thought he'd loved and how she had used him and tossed his love back in his face. "And I actually thought I could never love another woman for fear of getting hurt that way all over again, especially a female who was a city woman."

He chuckled in spite of himself, remembering the first night he'd seen her. "The moment I saw you I knew you were a city girl and as much as I didn't want to, I couldn't help falling in love with you anyway, Savannah."

He looked down at her, held her gaze. "And no matter what that document says, I do love you. I love you very much."

Savannah felt her cheeks getting wet and tried furiously to wipe at them. But Durango took over, and leaned down and licked them dry. When he pulled back his dark eyebrows rose, clearly astonished. "I thought all tears were salty but yours are sweet. Is there anything that's not perfect about you?"

Savannah let out a small cry and threw her arms around Durango's neck and whispered, "I love you, too, and I fell in love the exact moment that you did."

He chuckled softly and eased from the bed. "Then that leaves only one thing to do," he said, reaching to retrieve the legal document off the nightstand.

Savannah watched as he stood and walked over to the fireplace and tossed it in, and watched with him as the flames engulfed it, burning it to ashes.

"Now that is taken care of," he said.

Savannah kept her eyes on Durango as he slowly removed his shirt. Her heartbeat quickened when he then proceeded to take off his jeans. "I know you're probably too exhausted to make love, but I need to hold you in my arms, Savannah. I need your warmth, I need your love and I need your promise that you won't ever leave me."

She swallowed thickly when he came back to the bed and slipped under the covers with her. She turned to him when he pulled her into his arms. "I won't leave you, Durango. I want forever if you do…and I'm not tired."

He smiled. "I want forever, too, and you are tired. You just don't know it."

He captured her lips with his, kissing her with all the

intensity of a man who had found love by first having an affair—The Durango Affair. It was definitely his last.

"So, Mrs. Westmoreland, will you stay married to me? For better or for worse?"

She smiled through her tears. "Yes, I'll stay married to you, but I have a feeling all my days will be for the better."

He leaned over and kissed her after whispering, "I'll make sure of that."

Epilogue

Savannah glanced around the room. There were more Westmorelands than she remembered from Jessica's wedding. She'd known Durango's family was big but she had no idea it was this large.

The wedding reception given in their honor had turned out to be a beautiful affair. To Savannah's surprise, even her grandparents from Philly had come to be a part of it.

"I know how you feel," Dana Rollins Westmoreland eased up by her side to say. "The first time Jared took me to meet them I thought that this wasn't a family, it was a whole whopping village."

Savannah smiled, thinking the very same thing. She glanced around the room again and it was Tara Westmoreland, who was married to Durango's cousin Thorn, who came up and said, "It seems that Durango called a meeting with the menfolk."

"Oh," Savannah said, wondering the reason why.

Upon seeing her concern, Tara said, "I'm sure whatever they need to talk about won't take long. In the meantime, has anyone ever told you how I met Thorn?"

Savannah smiled. "No, but after meeting him I'm sure it was very interesting."

"Yes, it was. Come on, let me, you and Dana grab the others and go into the kitchen for a talk. If the guys can have a little chat time then so can we."

After gathering Delaney, Shelly, Madison, Jessica, Casey and Jayla up in their wake, the Westmoreland women headed for the kitchen. The married women would tell Savannah how they met their husbands and fell in love.

"Okay, I can see all of you have questions, so what is it you want to know?" Durango asked the men who had cornered him and demanded this meeting.

It was Stone who spoke up. "I know it's really none of our business, Durango, but we know you. What's the real reason you got married?"

Durango shook his head. He'd known his marriage would be hard for a lot of his family to believe, so he decided to be up-front with them, since he suspected a few had their suspicions anyway.

"Savannah is pregnant. However," he went on to say before unnecessary conversation could get started, "although her pregnancy might have been the reason we married initially, it's not now."

Spencer Westmoreland raised a dark eyebrow. "It's not?"

"No. I'm in love with her. She's in love with me. We're having a baby in September and we're happy."

The men in the room stared at him. A few, those who knew how easy it was to fall in love if the right woman came alone, accepted his words. But Durango saw a few skeptical gazes.

"And you want us to believe that just like that, a die-hard bachelor can fall in love?" Quade Westmoreland asked.

"It can happen," Durango said, smiling.

"I agree," added the man who'd once been such a confirmed bachelor that the women had pegged him the *Perfect Storm.* Storm Westmoreland met the gazes of his brothers and cousins and one lone brother-in-law, Sheikh Jamal Yasir. "All of you know my history and yet Jayla was able to capture my heart," he reminded them.

Thorn Westmoreland chuckled. "And all of you know what Tara did to me."

The men in the room doubted they would ever forget. Tara had been Thorn's challenge and had lived up to the task.

"And you're really happy about being married, Durango? No regrets?" Reggie Westmoreland asked, needing to be certain.

Durango met all the men's gazes. "Yes and there aren't any regrets. You've all seen Savannah. What man wouldn't be happy married to her? But her beauty isn't just on the outside. It's on the inside, as well. I need her in my life and she has single-handedly opened my heart to love."

All the men in the room finally believed him. As miraculous as it seemed, Durango Westmoreland had fallen in love. Unfortunately that didn't bode well for the remaining single Westmorelands, who didn't have falling in love on their agendas. The thought of doing so was as foreign to them as a six-legged bear.

"Congratulations and welcome to wedded bliss," Chase Westmoreland said, clapping Durango on the back.

"Thanks, Chase."

Other congratulations followed. It was Ian who had a serious question to ask. "What about us? The ones who have no desire to follow down that path?"

Durango grinned at his brother and said, "I hate to tell you this, but I doubt any man is safe. I'm going to tell it to you like someone older and wiser told it to me. No matter how much your heart is made of stone, it can turn to putty in the right woman's hands."

Jared Westmoreland grinned and raised his wineglass up in the air and said, "With that said, gentlemen, I rest my case."

Dare Westmoreland, who had been quiet all this time, smiled and said after glancing around the room at the remaining six Westmoreland bachelors, "Now we're faced with that burning question again. Which one of you will be next?"

* * * * *

Four sisters.
A family legacy.
And someone is out to destroy it.

A captivating new limited
continuity, launching June 2006

The most beautiful hotel in New Orleans,
and someone is out to destroy it. But mystery,
danger and some surprising family revelations
and discoveries won't stop the Marchand sisters
from protecting their birthright…
and finding love along the way.

SPECIAL PRICE!

This riveting new saga begins with

by national bestselling author

JUDITH ARNOLD

The party at Hotel Marchand is in full swing when the lights suddenly go out. What does head of security Mac Jensen do first? He's torn between two jobs—protecting the guests at the hotel and keeping the woman he loves safe.

A woman to protect. A hotel to secure. And no idea who's determined to harm them.

On Sale June 2006

Paying the Playboy's Price

(Silhouette Desire #1732)

by

EMILIE ROSE

Juliana Alden is determined to have her last—
her only—fling before settling down. And she's
found the perfect candidate: bachelor Rex Tanner.
He's pure playboy charm…but can she afford
his price?

Trust Fund Affairs: They've just spent a fortune—
the bachelors had better be worth it.

Don't miss the other titles in this series:

EXPOSING THE EXECUTIVE'S SECRETS (July)
BENDING TO THE BACHELOR'S WILL (August)

On sale this June from Silhouette Desire.

*Available wherever books are sold, including most
bookstores, supermarkets, discount stores and drugstores.*

COMING NEXT MONTH

#1729 HEIRESS BEWARE—Charlene Sands
The Elliotts
She was about to expose her family's darkest secrets, but then she lost her memory and found herself in a stranger's arms.

#1730 SATISFYING LONERGAN'S HONOR—Maureen Child
Summer of Secrets
Their passion had been denied for far too many years. But will secrets of a long-ago summer come between them once more?

#1731 THE SOON-TO-BE-DISINHERITED WIFE—Jennifer Greene
Secret Lives of Society Wives
He didn't know if their romantic entanglement was real, or a ruse in order to secure her multimillion-dollar inheritance.

#1732 PAYING THE PLAYBOY'S PRICE—Emilie Rose
Trust Fund Affairs
Desperate to break free of her good-girl image, this society sweetheart bought herself a bachelor at an auction. But what would her stunt really cost her?

#1733 FORCED TO THE ALTAR—Susan Crosby
Rich and Reclusive
Her only refuge was his dark and secretive home. His only salvation was her acceptance of his proposal.

#1734 A CONVENIENT PROPOSITION—Cindy Gerard
Pregnant and alone, she entered into a marriage of convenience… never imagining her attraction to her new husband would prove so *in*convenient.

SDCNM0506